Prince Lander and the Dragon War

Books by S. D. Smith

Publication Order:

The Green Ember
The Black Star of Kingston (The Tales of Old Natalia Book I)
Ember Falls: The Green Ember Book II
The Last Archer (Green Ember Archer Book I)
Ember Rising: The Green Ember Book III
The Wreck and Rise of Whitson Mariner (The Tales of Old Natalia Book II)
The First Fowler (Green Ember Archer Book II)
Ember's End: The Green Ember Book IV
The Archer's Cup (Green Ember Archer Book III)
Prince Lander and the Dragon War (The Tales of Old Natalia Book III)

Best read in publication order, but in general, simply be sure to begin with The Green Ember.

Prince Lander & the Dragon War

S. D. SMITH
ILLUSTRATED BY ZACH FRANZEN

Story Warren Books
www.storywarren.com

Copyright © 2022 by S. D. Smith

All rights reserved. No part of this publication may be reproduced, distributed, or transmitted in any form or by any means, including photocopying, recording, or other electronic or mechanical methods, without the prior written permission of the publisher, except in the case of brief quotations embodied in critical reviews and certain other noncommercial uses permitted by copyright law. This book is published under protest from the international coalition for the polite treatment of dragons. For permission requests, write to the publisher, addressed "Attention: Permissions Coordinator," at info@storywarren.com.

Trade Paperback edition ISBN: 978-1-951305-20-8
Also available in eBook and Audiobook.

Story Warren Books
www.storywarren.com

Cover and interior illustrations by Zach Franzen.
www.zachfranzen.com
Map created by Will Smith and Zach Franzen.

Printed in the United States of America
22 23 24 25 26   01 02 03 04 05

Story Warren Books
www.storywarren.com

To my father, H. Don Smith
and to my sons,
Josiah C. Smith and Micah E. Smith

For Dad

I am my father's son,
An heir who honors and remembers.
I do as he did,
As he called me to do.
I go on to build, not to collapse.
I am no tearer down,
But a builder on.
I am a faithful one.
I am my father's son.

For My Sons

Go on, boys,
I am blessing you, so go on.
I see you,
And I'm pleased with you.
I love you from my soul.
Follow your better Father,
And go farther,
Than you ever could by following me alone.
Go after me, but pass me.
Keep to the golden road,
But go beyond my utmost mark.
In my heart,
I am always with you.
So when you go beyond me,
I will, in some way,
Be there too.
When you were small I took you everywhere,
So take me with you, when you go,
In your heart.
Follow your better Father,
And go farther.
Go on, boys.
Go on.

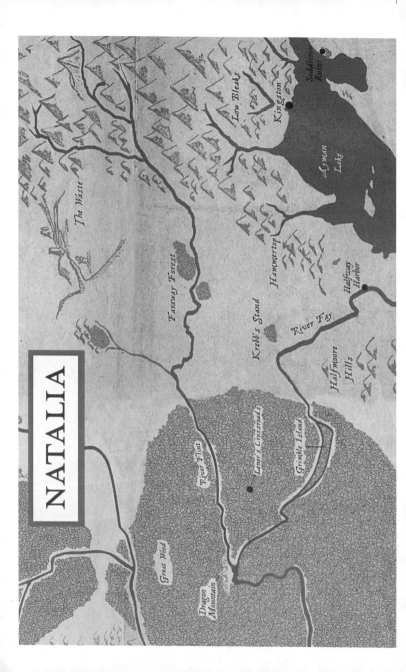

I saw the young prince fall at the edge of our camp. I know the dragon king's own blade carried his blood. We all mourned for him, but our king was ever after changed. We settled in to defend with all we had. I was there when the end really did come, when the fire we had feared threatened to consume all. In the end, it took so much. But I was gone when it took him.

From the Journal of Massie Burnson

Chapter One

Prince Lander flanked his father as they trudged forward in the snow, headed toward a shameful treaty with their bitter enemies.

"Get me Captain Massie!" King Whitson Mariner shouted back to his trailing train of officers and soldiers, his eyes unfocused as he limped along.

"Captain Massie is gone, Father," Prince Lander said, darting a worried look back through the falling snow at his brothers, Lemual and Grant. This was not the first time Father had asked for Captain Massie today. "It's been weeks, sir."

"Of course," King Whitson replied slowly, shaking his head as they halted. "I had forgotten a moment, son. Forgive me."

"It's nothing, Father," Lander replied, and he smiled as confidently as he was able to with honesty. It had been nearly two months since Doctor Grimes had told the family about King Whitson's affliction. Over time, the king would lose his power to think clearly. Before he reached old age, King Whitson's mind would waste away and he would die. Grief washed over Lander as he laid his hand on his father's shoulder. "Should we advance, sir? Lord Grimble will be waiting."

King Whitson coughed, looked around anxiously, then nodded. Grant, the brown-furred and barely of age fourth child of King Whitson and Queen Lillie, crossed his arms and spat. He grumbled, "If that oathbreaker Grimble somehow keeps his word this time."

Lemual, the short and slight-framed secondborn, shook his head, with a pleading look in his eyes and a nervous glance back toward their camp. Lander shrugged.

Prince Lander, the firstborn son and heir to King Whitson, agreed with his brothers and shared their worries. How could they go against everything their father had done for years? How could they leave the camp?

Prince Lander & the Dragon War

Lord Grimble wasn't to be trusted. He had proven that again and again. It had been many years since Grimble's first betrayal, back when Lander was only a child. But Lander was grown now, a seasoned veteran and a heroic captain of their kind. King Whitson, with what strength of mind and body he had remaining, insisted he was aiming to build an alliance that could defend and hold out against the dragons before his own end came. Whitson believed it was imperative to unite all the fractured rabbits of Natalia to accomplish this seemingly impossible task. Whitson's war plan came down to this call: *Defend all. All defend.* Yes, Lander agreed with his brothers that Grimble—a treacherous rabbit lord who had an alliance with the dragons—was not to be trusted. However, he also agreed with his father that their own band wasn't strong enough to defend against the dragons on their own.

A quandary.

Grant clenched and unclenched his fist over his sword hilt, agitation plain on his face. "Father! We absolutely *cannot* all go with you. We must keep a leader with a stronger force at camp."

Lander sighed. He knew this wouldn't help.

"Are you king now, Grant?" Whitson asked, his eyes flitting lazily around his senior officers. "Do you wish," he paused, looking around in confusion for a moment, then continued, "to argue yet again?"

"Father, no," Grant said, hurrying up beside him. "You are king and I'm your servant—"

"—my son," Whitson corrected. "My dear, dear son."

"Yes, Father," Grant replied. "I will follow you anywhere, of course. I'm not afraid to die, only—"

"Only you're certain you know better than a dimwitted oldster who can't remember what day it is or who is where half the time?"

"No, Father..."

Lander frowned. "Get back now, Grant. Leave Father to lead."

"You always say that," Grant hissed. "But one day this will fall to you, or Lemual, or me, and I don't want it to all be lost by then."

"Follow orders, Prince Grant," Lord Arben snapped. "Lord Grimble was right about you. You're a hotheaded fool and are sure to wreck everything!"

"Don't talk to him like that," Lemual said,

stepping forward as the officers and lords all spoke at once with raised, angry voices.

Whitson raised his hand for silence, then turned to his fourth-born son. "Grant Whitson, my dear buck." With an outstretched arm he beckoned his son to him, then slowly hooked his arm around Grant's shoulder. "You remind me of your grandfather. Lord Grant lived long on Golden Coast and came here with me, his son-in-law, and followed me loyally every day of his life in Natalia. He died defending our folk when you were knee-high. He knew what it meant to be a noble—to act nobly."

Lander hung his head. His Grandfather Grant had been precious to him. His death was an enduring wound and turned Lander's heart to thoughts of revenge against Lord Grimble. Lord Grant had died fighting Grimble's oathbreaking faction, not the dragons. The dragons had killed Lander's brother, Davis, yes. But both died following Father's uncompromising plan of defending their camp at all costs and with everything they had.

Grant shrugged. "Yes, Father. Isn't it our duty to protect our own, as he did?"

Whitson wiped at his mouth, then nodded. "What is the duty of a king?" he asked.

"To serve. To do rightly. To be first into danger and last out. To rule so that those under his rule are as free and good as they can possibly be."

"True. All of that is true." Whitson squeezed his son close, and his voice dropped lower. "He must also inspire them to follow, if he can. He must invite them to follow, if he cannot inspire them. And if he can do neither, he must insist that they follow."

Lander was close enough to hear. He saw Grant's eyes go from their father to the surrounding bucks—trusted officers and armed soldiers—many of whom had fought by Whitson's side since the beginning of his voyage.

Understanding dawned on Grant. He closed his eyes and exhaled. "Forgive me, Father. I will close my mouth and keep my place."

"It may comfort you to know this," Whitson whispered just loud enough for Lander to hear. "I have laid a trap for Grimble. You see, son, we have a traitor among our innermost councilors. I had to confirm some suspicions."

Grant's eyes grew wide. "If I have ruined that

Prince Lander & the Dragon War

plan, Father, I am mortified! Oh, Father, I am so sorry."

Whitson smiled. "You have not ruined it, son," he whispered. "You have carried it out."

Grant cocked his head sideways, and his mouth fell open, a perplexed expression on his face. But Lander smiled, his heart flooding with relief. *He knows who the spy is.*

"Prince Lander," Whitson said, turning swiftly. "Please arrest Lord Arben and Captain Danker. We do aim to make a treaty with Grimble, if he will see sense. But we will not be spied upon by him in the meantime."

Lander nodded toward Captain Rin. The captain and four of his bucks in the king's royal guard surrounded the traitors. Lander stepped forward. "I arrest you in the name of the king on suspicion of treason."

"You are making a treaty with Grimble, Your Majesty!" Lord Arben shouted. "It is not treason to merely converse with an ally."

"So you admit it?" Whitson snapped, seeming sharper than he had in weeks. "It is certainly treason to scheme with the king's enemies against him. It is certainly treason to conspire against your king. You know Grimble isn't keeping faith, and yet you aid him!"

"Drop your swords," Lander said, leveling his blade at Lord Arben's neck. Lord Arben didn't move, but Captain Danker slowly drew and dropped his blade. The weapon vanished beneath the snow, leaving a sword-shaped gash.

"Did you not suppose," King Whitson asked, stepping forward, "that if Grimble had a spy in my midst, I might have a spy in his? Did you not think that I might suspect you when you insisted that every senior officer and the bulk of our forces come to this treaty summit? Did you not think I would suspect when you inquired where the queen might be? He has stolen my Lillie once, with the aid of his dragon masters. I tell you today that he never shall again!"

Captain Danker fell to his knees and began babbling, begging forgiveness and promising to tell all.

"You old fool!" Lord Arben screamed, stepping forward. "You've lost your mind! You'll lose this war and lose all. We must make peace with the dragons as Lord Grimble has or else flee these lands forever!"

Whitson stepped closer and eyed him coldly. "Never."

Lord Arben's eyes grew wild, and he reached for his sword. Prince Lander's foot flashed out, kicking Arben's wrist hard. The furious buck opened his mouth to harangue the king further, but Prince Lander's open hand swiftly shot out to level the lord with a humiliating blow. The slap stunned him into silence.

Lander growled. "Take this traitor away."

As Lord Arben and Captain Danker were dragged off, King Whitson nodded to Lemual. "Take Captain Cove and find out what they know."

Prince Lemual nodded and, together with Captain Cove, hurried after the king's guards and their prisoners. Their crunching footfalls faded as the officers restored order.

"Well done, Your Majesty," Captain Walters said, crossing to bow to the king.

"We go to war on many fronts," Whitson replied, shaking hands with Walters. "I did truly long for a treaty with Grimble, of course, but I never thought it likely. We shall have to hope for aid from another place."

"Shall I re-form our usual defense, Your

Majesty?" Walters asked.

"At once, if you please, Captain," the king replied. "Until help comes, we must defend all. And all must defend."

"What if Massie never returns?" Grant asked.

"Are you still so full of doubts, my son?"

Grant winced. "Forgive me, Father. I feel I am always about to let you down with my foolishness."

"You *feel*, Grant," Whitson said, "and that is your great strength—and weakness. Feeling without thought is wild, but thought without feeling is not alive. Keep being alive, son."

Lander shook his head at Grant. "Maybe one day you'll be alive long enough to grow a brain."

Grant held up his hands, accepting the gibe.

There was noise through the ranks, and Lander gazed down the long train of soldiers till he saw a messenger making his way up the line. He sagged onto a snowbank, then staggered ahead, leaning on the helping arms of soldiers along the way.

"This might be bad," Lander groaned.

"We are at war," Grant said, "so even my tiny brain knows this isn't good."

Lander stepped between the stumbling messenger and the king.

The young rabbit bowed, the badly bandaged gash on his head bleeding freely. "If you please, Your Highness, a report."

"Go ahead, soldier."

"We were ambushed, sir. I was the only one to get away."

"Medic!" Lander shouted, as the injured

messenger fell to his knees. "There, son," Lander whispered, taking the young buck's bleeding head in his hands as the soldiers stepped closer. "We're going to get you taken care of, soldier."

"Your Highness," the messenger said, tears in his eyes, "Grimble's faction are doing it again. They are trading half their younglings to renew their alliance with the dragons."

Lander's chest tightened, and he felt a sickening constriction in his throat. "When?" he growled.

"At dawn, my lord," the messenger whispered hoarsely. Then his eyes rolled back as he collapsed fully into the prince's arms.

Chapter Two

Hours later, as darkness fell fully, Prince Lander's raft landed on the edge of Grimble Island. As he scrambled off the raft, his leg dragged in the icy river. Suppressing a cry, he rubbed vigorously at the leg, freeing his fur of most of the freezing water. But it had soaked into his foot wrapping, undoing its intended protection. *Worse things than cold feet will happen if I don't hurry on.* Shivering, he glanced back to see Captain Walters on the other shore, his rounded belly standing out in a moonlit silhouette. He stood ready to launch his larger boats when signaled. Lander pulled the raft onto the beach and crept ahead.

He had expected sentinels. He had prepared for them. Bow in hand and quiver bouncing gently behind him, he ran along the crunching snow to the cover of the tree line and crouched low. Peering through the darkness and the falling snow, he saw no sign of Grimble's soldiers. He ran ahead, knowing the way from careful study of the map. And, of course, he had been here before.

Years ago, Captain Grimble had taken his fallen father's place as lord and leader of the Grimble faction—*oathbreakers* is how Lander and his larger community of loyalist rabbits thought of them. Lander hadn't come onto the island itself since then, but he had been through a harrowing adventure there with Captain Massie the day they first discovered the dragons and rescued Queen Lillie.

Now the dragons had given the island to Lord Grimble and only reserved their sacred pool at its center for their dark rituals. Grimble's faction ruled the island, often allying with the dragon king's army to defend it from incursions by King Whitson's loyalist forces. Lander peered into the forest, now caked with snow, and recognized where he must go. He began to walk, his wrapped feet sinking into the deepening snow.

A sound from behind startled him, and he

Prince Lander & the Dragon War

darted for a snow-covered bush. *Steps.* Closer, and closer.

Lander sprang up and leveled a nocked arrow at a creeping form.

"Yer Highness-ness," the shrouded shape whispered through a muffled mask.

"Identify!" Lander snapped.

"I'm Nickel," he said, open hands out to show they were free of weapons. "Here, Yer Royal H, to see that ye are not killed."

Lander lowered his bow, recognizing the lanky form of Nickel Drekker. "What's wrong with you? You're jeopardizing a mission here, young Nickel. Who ordered you to follow me?"

"I only ordered myself, Yer Highness-ness," he said, shrugging.

"That's not how this works," Lander hissed. "Go back the way you came."

"Who then might have yer back, sir?" Nickel asked.

"I'm doing this alone," Lander explained, "because it's not a job for a band. And I'm doing it alone so I don't have to guide an impertinent, inexperienced buck through the whole thing. Walters is my backup, and I planned—Listen, I don't need to explain this to you. I need you to follow orders!"

"I will, to be sure, my good prince and lord. But if ye will indulge me, just one last question. Did ye spot them two archers in yon high nests ahead?"

"What?" Lander spun and ducked down, gazing up through the thickening fall of snow.

"They'll be waiting, sir," Nickel said, "for ye to do what ye were about to do. Just clamber through that clearing and right into their trap."

Lander scanned the trees and finally spotted them, two archers hidden high with a commanding view of the clearing. His heart dropped. He would be dead were it not for Nickel's intervention. In his anger and eagerness, he had rushed ahead foolishly. *Maybe I'm not so different from Grant.* Nodding his thanks to Nickel, Lander remembered the strange skill set of this young soldier. He was a little mouthy and in trouble often, yes, but he also had an uncanny ability with a sling. He and a few of his cousins were actually training a cohort of soldiers in this archaic craft passed down from his ancestors. Nickel also wore a unique shield on his back, narrow at the bottom but widening at the top

Prince Lander & the Dragon War

and plated in metal. Lander had to acknowledge that, for all his problems, Nickel was an effective soldier. "You can stay, Nickel. But follow my lead, and don't talk."

"Of course, Highness. I barely say a word ever, anyways. I'm a quiet sort of feller and modest as a tottering old codger what's lost his chompers."

"Nickel!" Lander snapped. "Be quiet."

"Aye, my lord," Nickel replied, placing a hand over his mouth.

"But do speak up," Lander amended, "and point out anytime I'm about to be killed."

Nickel bowed with a playful flourish of his right hand and, sliding the long shield from his back, crossed to the prince's side.

Lander raised his bow, sighting the distant archer nestled in the high tree on the left. "You ready, Nickel?"

"Aye, sir," he replied, setting a carved stone in his sling. "Ready to roar."

Lander rose and fired. A screaming curse sounded from the high tree, followed by a falling form. An arrow raced at Lander, but Nickel lunged, and his shield deflected it away.

Lander pivoted, nocked another shaft, and

fired in a swift motion as he reloaded again. The arrow missed, and the enemy rabbit began scrambling down the tree. Lander sprang ahead.

Plowing through the snow, Lander heard Nickel's swift steps behind him. The younger buck soon dashed past him and quickly closed on the sentinel. Lander squinted against the snow and saw the enemy trudge through a windblown snowdrift, driving ever closer to Grimble's camp, where he would give the alarm. When Nickel reached the snowdrift, he didn't slow down for a second but leapt over it with seeming ease. He landed in a small clearing and set his sling swinging. The agile weapon whirled as the young buck sped along. The enemy was about to disappear into the forest when Nickel let loose his stone. The rock raced ahead and, just as the fleeing guard swiveled back to check his pursuit, struck him hard. He fell, feet flying into the air, in a sliding wreck that shaped a long trench in the snow.

Lander jogged up, breathing hard, and found Nickel bent over the fallen form. "Did you get him?"

"Aye, sir," Nickel said. "He'll trouble us no more—nor them young ones below, if ye and me have our say tonight."

Prince Lander nodded and, breathing hard, paused on the rocky edge of a precipice. The settlement below was laid out just as their spy had said. A large barn stood on the far side of the town—the one in which they kept the younglings penned on such horrific nights. This was the cost of Grimble's grotesque alliance with King Namoz, lord of dragons.

"One concern I have is that these younglings won't want to come with us if they realize who we are," Lander said. "They've been trained to hate Whitson's loyalists since birth."

"And them wretched malefactors will have no doubt told them kids nothing about what their fate is."

"We have to save them," Lander said. "We can't let them go to the dragons."

Behind them, a rising noise. Fast, crunching footfalls approached.

Chapter Three

Lander spun, nocking an arrow in an instant.

"Yer Highness-ness, hold," Nickel said, stepping in front of the aimed arrow. "I'm next to certain these midnight marauders are me own band."

Lander sighed, lowering the bow and spinning back to check the fortified town below the cliff on which they stood. There was a clearing to their left and a long stone stairway leading down to a wall surrounding the town. "Your own band?"

"Aye, that." Nickel whistled a rhythmic repeating tune. It came back to him with an answering flourish from the trees behind them. "That'll be me sister."

"Your sister?" Lander winced and shook his

head. "Send her back!"

Nickel shrugged. "Very headstrong, that one."

"Must run in the family."

Nickel shrugged again, then spun to greet his sister, who jogged up with a carefree smile and open arms. Behind her followed five more bucks, no doubt all related to the odd twins. Lander recognized her. Winnie Drekker was her name, and she was as troublesome as her brother, but both were among the friendliest of their odd clan. Lander believed she might be some kind of inventor, but he wasn't certain. The five bucks were silent and wore bemused expressions. A large number of their semi-nomadic band had come to Natalia with Whitson, but the Drekkers had a complicated history with the old kings and community of Golden Coast. That continued in Natalia.

The four major places in the long history of rabbitkind were well-known. Their mythology began on Immovable Mountain—the place left by Flint and Fay—when they and the Leapers crossed to Blue Moss Hills. From Blue Moss Hills, long years later, the Trekkers journeyed for many years until they finally found Golden Coast. When, centuries after that, Golden Coast

Prince Lander & the Dragon War

was threatened with invasion and annihilation, Whitson Mariner and a host of survivors took to the seas. They sailed in a vast company of ships across the sea to Natalia, where they now strove for a home. Prince Lander, King Whitson and Queen Lillie's first child, had been born in Natalia. Nickel and Winnie's family were part of a group called the Dead Trekkers—usually now shortened to Drekkers—a community that came to Golden Coast many years after the original Trekkers who made the long voyage from Blue Moss Hills. They had been assumed dead, so when they showed up hundreds of years later at the thriving kingdom of Golden Coast, they found an uneasy welcome, and the separate cultures clashed. Lander's father had told him many stories of the Drekkers' odd interactions with old King Gerrard and the lords. Nickel and Winnie's parents, along with dozens of other Drekkers, had joined the voyagers fleeing Golden Coast with Whitson Mariner, but they had maintained a kind of independent culture among those loyal rabbits. Many thought they might join with Grimble's oathbreakers, but the Drekkers had so far kept faith with Whitson.

Nickel Drekker nodded to Winnie. "Sister, ye well?"

"Aye, well," Winnie replied. "His Yer Highness," she said, bowing quickly to Prince Lander. Her band followed her and bowed their short bows.

"Winnie Drekker," Lander said, keeping his voice level, "you and your band must return to the mainland and then get back to the village."

"Aye, sir," she replied, "but may I ask ye just one teensy-weensy question first?" She didn't wait for his response. "Suppose we had a scheme that'd keep ye alive and, added to that, would help ye save them poor younglings yonder this cold night?"

Lander turned his head and gazed at the trees, expecting another ambush thwarted. Seeing nothing, he sighed and turned back. "I suppose I would listen to that before you left. But the moon is rising soon, and we have to hurry. What's your scheme?"

Winnie laughed. "I don't have no scheme, Highness, but Nick'll have ten."

Nickel smiled and nodded. "Eight for now, but give me two shakes and I'll have ye three more."

"That's eleven, that," said one of the cousins.

Nickel laughed. "Promise'm coal and deliver'm gold."

Lander frowned. "Is that an old Drekker saying handed down from centuries past?"

"No," Nickel replied, "I've just come out with it, but it'll go the other way 'round now and get remembered for centuries hence-ahead."

"Or," Winnie put in, "forgotten tomorrow's the more like."

Nickel shook his head. "She's been this way since infancy, that one. Doubting the enduring quality of me pithy wisdom. It's a load on me mind, sure."

"About them eleven schemes," Winnie said.

Lander gazed at the horizon. "We just need one. But we need it soon. It's one hour till this place gets a lot brighter."

Nickel nodded. "I'll start with me worst, then ye will have a range to—"

Lander held up a hand. "Start with your best, Nickel."

"Aye, sir," he replied. "I hope ye like it. It's a trick."

* * *

An hour later, Lander watched from the other side of the town while the moon rose behind the cliffside they had just left. Nickel and Winnie looked over at Lander, eyes wide with a question. Lander glanced across the valley and saw fifty forms perched on the illuminated horizon. The moon glowed behind the cliffside forms and shone into the town the Grimbles had built, with its forts and mills, watchtowers and houses. The houses were spare; many were mere hovels. Lander again spied the watchtower, its bell outlined high in its top, where—strangely—no guard watched. The prince nodded, and Nickel nodded back, then passed the nod on to his sister and their cousins down the line.

Lander rose and aimed an arrow, remembering his training from Captain Massie. *Where are you now, Captain?* He fired at the tower bell, and it struck with an echoing peal. Rocks from loosed slings rained down on rooftops, and the eight rabbits hidden on the rim of town began shouting wildly.

Soon the town's rabbits rushed from forts and homes, tripping into the lanes and grabbing for weapons. They gazed up at the hillside where the hidden rabbits' shouts echoed off the rock and seemed to originate. Outlined against the moon, the forms of rabbit warriors stood poised in attack, with terrible weapons ready to wreak havoc. The Grimble soldiers, mustering in haste and charging up the hill, didn't have the clarity to pause and watch the frozen forms. They didn't see, until they were upon the would-be attackers on the moonlit ridge, that the rabbit soldiers they attacked were stationary. They were harmless—made of snow.

Meanwhile, Lander and the Drekker twins rushed over the wall and into the town. They darted for the nearby barn that served as the holding pen for the children set aside for the dragons. Throwing over the large wooden beam barring the door, they charged inside. The frightened children huddled along the far wall. Winnie and Lander called out orders. "This way, younglings!"

In front of the frightened crowd, an older child—nearly of age—stood with her arms out and fists clenched in front of the others. "I know what you're doing!" she shouted. "I know about the bargain with the dragons! I'll fight you!"

When Lander reached them, his hands open and outstretched, she threw a fast jab at his stomach. Caught off guard, he felt the blow hit home. He coughed and reached for her.

"Look at us!" Lander said. He grabbed her arms and forced her to look at his face. "Do I look familiar? Does she?" he asked, pointing at Winnie.

Weeping now, it took her a few moments to stop and look. Still sobbing, but with a look of new fear in her eyes, she shook her head.

Lander's voice was steady. "We're from Whitson's army." She began thrashing away, but he held her tight. "You have heard many lies about us, I'm sure, but look into my eyes and hear this. We pay no tribute to the dragons. We protect and cherish all our young. And we've come to rescue you."

The young doe was speechless with confusion and fear, and her eyes darted between the strangers and the young she had vowed to protect. "I, I, I…"

"It's all right, there," Winnie said. "We got to get moving. Can ye help us lead these younger ones away? I see they look to ye. They trust ye. Ye could save them this night, if ye will only act fast."

Lander thought he understood the possible story of how this older doe got in with these other, very young, ones. She had learned, somehow, of what the leaders planned. Indignant that her elders would turn over younglings to the dragons, she either defied them and was thrust in here with them or she volunteered to join them and share their terrible fate. Either way, Lander admired her courage. But now she was struggling, and they were running out of time. The ruse on the hillside with the warrior snow rabbits would have been discovered by now. The oathbreaker defenders, perhaps Lord Grimble himself and his most deadly soldiers, would be rushing back to discover what mischief was afoot in their town. Part of Lander relished the confrontation. An agonizing memory of Grimble killing Lord Grant, Lander's own dear grandfather, was seared into his memory. *I'd like a chance to settle that score—and many others.* Shaking his head, he saw that Winnie was trying to help the young doe understand while Nickel crept to the edge of the crowd and calmed the most upset.

"Ye can lead these to safety with us," Winnie said.

The young doe fell to her knees, hands pressed over her mouth as her eyes grew wide with panic. She seemed trapped between two evil choices, and she was choking on the moment. Her breathing thickened and she sagged, but Lander held her up. He smiled at her. "It's all right, dear. You're going to be okay, and so are all of them. What's your name?"

"I'm Hollie," she whispered. "Hollie Grimble."

Chapter Four

Hollie Grimble. *Grimble? Grimble!* Lander stepped back, a sudden anger stirring in his chest.

"Come on, now," Winnie said, pulling Hollie to her feet. She turned to the prince. "We best get gone, sir."

Grimble!

Lander glared at Hollie a moment, then nodded. "Let's go!"

Lander dashed out the open door, and Winnie, one hand gripping Hollie's and the other waving for the rest to follow, hurried after him. Nickel, sling at the ready in one hand, nudged the last of the younglings to follow.

Winnie turned. "Hurry, now! Move and go!"

she called, clicking her tongue at them. "All's gonna be good soon if ye'll hurry yer bottoms on."

They ran. Lander, recovering from his alarm at discovering he was rescuing his enemy's own daughter, stepped into the moonlit street. Angry shouts echoed from the ridge above, and noise swelled in nearby lanes.

Nickel was leading the younglings over the wall with the clever steps he'd hastily improvised half an hour before. Up and over the wall went the line of rescued young rabbits. Lander, his bow nocked and his heart racing, stood alongside a sling-wielding Winnie as they covered the escape.

A backward glance told Lander the last youngster was over, and he nodded for Winnie to follow. She spun and ran, bounding over the wall in two easy leaps. Lander, a bit older and a lot more wary, took a more cautious approach. But both cleared the wall and, landing on the packed snow, found the party far up the hillside. The small ones were running, hurried on by Hollie's encouragement. She had found her voice, and, though Lander could see in her backward glances that she was far from pleased to be in the company of Whitson's rabbits, she was making the best of their limited options and helping the little ones move quickly.

Soon they were deep into the forest and halfway to the shoreline. Safety loomed ahead.

"Oh!" Hollie cried. Lander jogged near enough to see a small buck, so young he hadn't been walking very long, collapse in the snow. Hollie bent and tended to him, urging the others to hurry on and follow Nickel.

Lander, stepping closer and darting glances back toward the town, slung his bow back over his shoulder. "There's no time."

Hollie's face hardened. "Then I'll stay here and die with him," she snapped back.

Lander smiled and bent low, scooped up the buck, and hurried ahead. "Come on, Hollie Grimble. We're leaving no one behind. Not even you."

Lander heard the crunch of snow behind them as Hollie jogged on. Soon she passed him and rushed to help the last stragglers of the group keep up the grueling run. The last one, staggering a few steps, veered off the path and began to fall. Hollie reached for her and soon was running again, the small doe clinging to her and hooked onto her hip. In a few minutes, they had to slow their pace at the back of the line. Lander ordered Nickel to carry on up front with the fastest, while Winnie, Hollie, and he urged on the slowest ones. Soon Lander was carrying three younglings, while Hollie and Winnie bore two each. But they pressed on, gasping out encouraging commands as they struggled to keep up.

Winnie tripped and fell, protecting the two she carried as well as she could as she rolled in the snow. She breathed in and out deeply, holding up her hand. Then she coughed, took them up again, and pressed on.

"A little farther," Lander called, "just a little bit farther."

"You said that...ten minutes ago," Hollie said, panting.

"It's even...truer...now," he gasped.

A shout came from behind—the sound of distant rushing and cries. Lander's heart sank.

"They found us," Hollie screamed. "Father will kill us all!"

"Run!" Lander cried, forcing his aching legs to go on.

An arrow raced between his ears, and he stumbled, almost losing his footing. But he dug in and sprinted ahead, his lungs burning, his legs wobbling, and his heart thumping hard and fast.

More arrows. More again. Lander saw it all in moonlit flashes: dark blurry lines against a pale white background, stabbing into snowy ground and sticking suddenly into trees.

They will catch us. They will kill them all. I have to slow them down.

"Can you run a bit now?" Lander asked the three little ones he carried. They cried. "When I set you down you must run after the others. Follow Hollie. Now!" He slowed and set them down while arrows raced overhead. They did rush forward, and he desperately hoped it was fast enough. He spun back, gasping as he unslung his bow.

Lander nocked three arrows and fired at the dark forms crashing through the woods in pursuit. He forced his burning arms to reach and clench three more and fired again as more arrows sank into trees all around him, nipping the fur of his face and splitting the edge of his winter cloak. Now he drew a single shaft, picked his enemy, and sent it crackling at him. The oathbreaker fell with a cry just before an arrow found Lander's leg, spinning him down. He hadn't thought his legs could be in any more pain than they had been, but he was wrong. In agony, he knelt and drew his bow again, determined to take out as many enemies as possible before the end. Nocking his long dart with determination, he scanned the attackers for a likely target—hoping to see Grimble himself. Settling on a forward buck shouting orders and urging his force ahead, Lander squinted.

The buck lurched back, staggered, and fell dead. Lander blinked and glanced down at his unshot arrow.

Then arrows were flying overhead the other way, and his enemies were spinning down, crying out, and falling back. The trees around Lander burst with loyal bucks, pressing ahead to rescue their prince and cover the escape of the younglings.

Lander launched his arrow, adding to the rally, then fell back onto the snow. A medic knelt and assessed his leg. Soon two strong bucks were hauling him back toward the shore. For a moment he almost ordered them to set him down. Instinct called him to stay in the fight. But he had learned through many battles that sometimes brave and foolish acts like that got good bucks killed and only satisfied a captain's vanity. He thanked the soldiers bearing him and let them do their job. As they cut through the last row of trees and the shoreline spread out in the moonlight, he saw the last of the little ones being welcomed into a boat. Hollie Grimble handed that last little doe in, then carefully stepped in herself as they shoved off.

The plan had worked. Grimble's perverse bargain had been undone. The little ones would live.

For now.

The dragon king, Namoz the Destroyer, would be livid.

Lander was lifted onto a boat and joined there by a medic as soldiers surrounded the beach.

"Your Highness," the medic said after a more careful examination by torchlight, "I think you'll come out of this well. It's lodged deep, sir, but managed to miss anything that might have killed you. I've cleaned it, and we'll treat it more thoroughly when we get back to camp."

"If we have time for that," Lander said, gritting his teeth. Seeing the medic's puzzled expression, he continued. "I wonder if, after years of skirmishes and raids, retaliation and slow, simmering animosity, we've finally tipped the thing into the all-out war we knew would someday come."

"Aye," the medic said. "As your father the king has been saying for years, sir, we must 'be ready to defend and defend and defend, for the final war will come—someday.'"

Lander gazed back toward Grimble Island as their boat rowed for the opposite shore. "I think someday might be here."

Chapter Five

Lander lay still on a table while Doctor Grimes stitched his wound. "Your Highness, I have a salve for the pain," she said.

"Thank you, no," Lander replied, smiling with teeth clenched. "I know we have a shortage, and there are worse wounds to come."

"Does it hurt badly, son?" King Whitson's firelit face showed concern.

"Yes," Lander said, winking at his mother as he strained.

Queen Lillie smiled as she sewed. When she wasn't at her desk working through manuscripts—just now her desk was piled high with books and neatly stacked papers—she was busy sewing warm cloaks for soldiers. "That's good, son. It takes more

strength to be honest than to lie in a misguided effort at toughness."

"In my day," Father said, frowning at Mother, "we'd outdo each other in exaggerating how fine we were."

"I have two problems with that," Mother replied, setting down her sewing. "One is that it rarely helps to lie. Inviting others who are strong into our genuine pain is a sign of respect and can be a gift." This was an old argument. Lander listened and tried not to squirm under the stitching, which was agonizing. "And two," the queen continued, "*your day* is not done. There is no 'back in my day,' my dear husband and king. It is your day *now*."

Whitson's gaze flicked from the fire to his son's wounded leg. "I am not so ruined as I put on recently to flush out the spies—thank you, my dear wife, for that brilliant scheme—but I feel it. I am not as strong as I once was. The end will come, as Doctor Grimes here has made clear."

Lander exchanged a glance with the elderly doctor who had cared for his family as long as he'd been alive. She smiled sadly.

"You seem older every year, Father," Lander said, then exhaled slowly as the last stitch went home.

Whitson chuckled. "You have your mother's wit, Lander. But I do feel the years piling on me. I feel on the brink of…" He trailed off.

Doctor Grimes coughed, conscious of being in the middle of an honest family conversation, and gathered up her tools. "It'll heal, Your Highness, but you must stay off it for a week at least."

"Thank you," Lander replied, making no promises. The doctor knew that what she asked was unlikely, and she sighed as she turned toward the door. "Your Majesties," she said, bowing. "I will bring your memory tonic tomorrow, sir," she said, nodding to the empty bottle by Whitson's desk. "I see you are out."

"Ah, yes," Father replied.

Doctor Grimes frowned. "You know, sir, that taking more than the dose I prescribed will give no additional benefit. And it only means I must give you more of your, uh, other medicine."

"Of course," Whitson said, carefully avoiding both the doctor's and Queen Lillie's gaze, "thank you ever so much." The old doe bowed again and left.

Lander slid off the table and tested his step. "That'll be tough to run on."

Queen Lillie started to speak but stopped, shook her head, and continued sewing.

Lander smiled at the queen. "You have advice for your foolish son, Mother?"

Queen Lillie looked at Lander with affection. "Take care of yourself, as much as you're able to, son. We will need you to be strong."

Prince Lander & the Dragon War

Lander's grin disappeared, and he bowed. "Yes, Mother. I will obey."

"The final war to defend our camp approaches, son," Father said. "And thanks to your heroics, we now have more vulnerable ones to defend than ever."

"We're very proud of you, Lander," Mother said, biting off a piece of thread.

Father nodded. "Aye, very proud indeed. Go farther than I have gone, Lander. Go on and do better. I know you will be a great king, my dear son—if we can somehow survive."

"If we do not survive," Mother said, "we will go down and die as we have lived. Survival is not the ultimate aim. Our beloved Davis died defending this camp, and we may follow his good example. Grimble is paying too high a price to ensure his faction's mere survival."

"It's not his own blood he pays in," Lander growled. "I'd like to…" He trailed off, shaking his head as he stepped slowly around the room.

Father exhaled through clenched teeth. "I still believe we must make peace with him, somehow. If we hope to defend rabbitkind, we must have more soldiers."

"We have allies," Mother said.

Whitson shrugged. "We don't know if anyone besides us has survived. For all we know, it's the oathbreakers and us. Alone against the dragons. And they aren't even against the dragons, yet."

"They're likely to be angrier at us than ever," Lander said, "after the rescue."

Mother nodded. "I have to hope that many of them are secretly relieved we've saved their own children."

Whitson paced up and down the small lodging. "Maybe it's our chance. Maybe we hold a summit now. Maybe they fear the dragons' anger and will come over to our side. Maybe one of the older bucks, like Captain Salno, will speak reason to Grimble."

Lander shook his head. "I expect not, Father. I fear they will use this as an excuse to make a final attack."

"I had hoped this cruel winter would slow the dragons down," Whitson replied. "And it has, some. But not enough. They still seem to move with astonishing agility. If they attacked, we would have no chance. We *must* have reinforcements."

"If you like, Father, I'll go back to the island under a flag of truce," Lander said. "I'll parley with Grimble and set another meeting. We can try."

Mother frowned.

Father rubbed at his eyes. Lander's heart ached, seeing the weight of decision on his father's haggard face. He was changing. The dreaded day approached when Whitson Mariner would be king no more. If Doctor Grimes' forecast was true—and he had never known her to be wrong about such things—the end was not far off. Lander blinked away tears as the king crossed to the fire and held his hands out toward it. Lander exchanged a worried glance with his mother.

Father spoke into the silence. "I feel myself weakening. I don't know what to do."

Lander started to speak, to fill the uncomfortable silence with a reassuring response. But his mother's face deterred him. She sat in the sadness, silent. She felt it all but did not rush to talk over it. *This is real. This is happening.*

Lander could think of only one thing—the thing perhaps his father would finally be open to using as a last resort.

"Father, maybe it's time to bring it out. Maybe it's time to unbury the starsword."

Chapter Six

Whitson gazed into the fire. He did not reply but only shook his head.

Mother spoke in a whisper. "There's a good reason why your father buried it. It's too powerful for anyone to use and not be changed."

The unspoken thing hung between them. Lander almost said it. *Maybe Father needs to be changed.*

The starsword was buried in a box, and he knew exactly where. Few knew of its existence—fewer still that Whitson had recovered it from the wreck of the *Vanguard*. Not for the first time, Lander thought of going to that secret place, digging the ancient sacred blade up, and giving it a trial on Grimble's faction and their dragon allies.

"It's Flint's own sword, Father," Lander whispered. "He struck down Firstfoe with it, didn't he? He used it to preserve our kind at the beginning. Should we not use it to prevent rabbitkind's end?"

Whitson did not turn around. His voice was even but strained at the edges. "I keep almost nothing from you, son. But this one thing I have. I haven't wanted to add to the burden you carry as bearer of the Green Ember."

Lander looked over at Mother. She stared at the seam of the cloak she sewed, but her hands did not move. "I want to hear, Father. If it will ease the burden on you."

"I know you do, son," Father replied. He paused a moment, gazing into the flames. "It's the blade, son. Every night since I touched the sword—since I held it in my hand—I have dreamed the same dream. This is why I have never touched it once since that first day. In my dream, I take the starsword from its hiding place, and I kill every enemy myself—including Grimble and King Namoz. It works perfectly, and I work perfectly with it. It is spectacular. I win. We win." He paused a long moment.

Lander's frustration grew. "Then why, Father—"

"That's not how the dream ends, son," Whitson continued. "After we win, I keep the sword. I can't give it up. I use it more, and more, and more. I kill and kill—everyone, everywhere. I am alone with my sword at the end. I am worse than any oathbreaker or monster we've faced. The last part of the dream is me looking into a mirror and seeing that I have...I have become a dragon, myself."

Lander sat down heavily. "Every night, Father?"

"Yes."

Lander looked at Mother. She glanced sadly at Father, then back at Lander. She nodded toward the piles of books and journals on her desk. "I believe the story we have of Flint may not be complete. There are parts of Fay's book that warn of a cost for carrying the blade. She doesn't say what happened, but some wise ones—among them, our beloved Mother Saramack—believe that Flint's fall was connected with the use of the starsword. When the dreams started, I began to study the book more seriously alongside several of our best scholars."

"What does it say?" the prince asked, heart racing.

S. D. Smith

"Much, son," Mother replied. "It is a storehouse of history and wisdom. It includes so much that must be carefully guarded for the present."

"More burdens," Lander groaned.

"More responsibilities, yes," she replied. "More sacred charges. Like the younglings you rescued. Our duty isn't easy, but it is ours to defend and protect."

Lander bowed. "What have you found out about the sword?"

"They tried to break it," King Whitson replied. "I think that's why our kings kept it and kept it secret. Not to use, but to one day figure out how to destroy it. There are warnings passed down that we've only just rediscovered."

Lander held up his empty hands. "Did King Gerrard warn you in person when they made you king?"

Whitson shrugged. "He said the sword was a deadly relic his father had kept hidden, and he had too. I'm not sure he knew what was meant by 'deadly.' The warnings were lost—or ignored—down the line of kings. As Golden Coast prospered, fewer studied the old words or heeded the old warnings."

Lander sat down and rubbed his hands together. "So, when Fay says the sword's eventual breaking means the beginning of the mending, it might mean that the sword itself needs to break so that a mending is possible?"

Mother frowned. "We don't know. We only know that Fay warned against its overuse, and we know your father has had this dream these many years since he held it. Repeated specific dreams mean things. That's clear. What it means for the starsword, we are trying to uncover."

"I fear that, in the end, the user may be used by it," Father said. "Perhaps that's what happened to Flint Firstking. But more searching is needed in Fay's book and our other ancient sources. Mother Saramack is studying it all now—has been for a long time. Mother and I will go see her tonight, and she will update us on her progress. Maybe there's more about the starsword."

Lander sighed, then rose and crossed to his father. "I'm sorry."

"It's a hard thing not to take it up. I long to have it in my hands again. It could be a weapon that changes our odds. I don't know, but the possibility haunts me."

Prince Lander & the Dragon War

Lander embraced his father. He felt the hard Ruling Stone pressing between his father's chest and his own. Around Lander's neck hung the Green Ember, a sign of his role as next to rule. He had borne this for most of his life and had thought that he knew and shared all his father's burdens. But there were more—always more. And Mother, too, had secrets that he did not know. The sword and the book. The endless burdens of rule.

He sat on the couch near the fire, thinking of what he should say. His eyes grew heavy, and his thoughts blurred. "Father, I'm proud to be your son."

Whitson took Lander's hand and squeezed it. Then he pulled the blanket off the couch's back, eased his son down, and covered him. "I'm not tired," Lander said.

He did sleep. Later, loud, rapid knocks sounded, and Lander woke quickly and sat up. Grant hurried inside. He bowed quickly to Father and Mother. "If you please, sir. Dragons spotted on the west ridge."

Lander lurched ahead and nearly fell, forgetting his injury for a moment. Whitson caught him, and Grant rushed forward to assist. "I'm fine, thank you," Lander said, steadying on his own. He saw the dawn light coming through the open door behind Grant.

"How many?" Father asked.

"At least six," Grant replied.

"Prepare five teams to head to the east ridge," Father said, "and two for the west."

Grant hesitated a moment, a question forming on his lips. Then he bowed neatly, said, "Aye, sir," and rushed out.

King Whitson reached for his sword—his ordinary sword—and strapped it on.

Chapter Seven

Lander was tasked with securing the camp while Grant and their father led the two units west and east, respectively.

"Your Highness," Captain Cove said, saluting as he ran up to Lander. "The camp is secure. We have extra guards north and south. Prince Lemual leads the south party, as you ordered."

"Thank you, Captain." Lander handed him a skin of water.

"Much obliged, sir."

"Be honest, Captain Cove. Are the soldiers worried about Father?"

"That he's sent more than twice our forces where the enemy ain't been spotted, sir?" Cove asked.

"Yes."

"Some are, sir," Cove replied. "But not the veterans. We've been with him these many years. Ever since Grimble took the queen and the old *Vanguard* was wrecked, he's been wise to their schemes and thwarted them at their deceptions."

"You pulled him out of the water that day, Captain," Lander said, "and went on to steer the *Steadfast* through the treacherous rapids. Helmer, indeed. You saved us many times in those days, and many times since. I'm grateful for your loyalty, sir."

"Your father made me what I am," he replied, "and I'm a kingsbuck forever."

"Have you seen Winnie Drekker?"

"Aye, sir," Cove replied, frowning as he peered around. "I ordered her to report to you at once, just as you asked. But, she...uh..."

"She doesn't follow orders well?" Lander shook his head. "I understand, believe me. Carry on, Captain."

Captain Brindle "Helmer" Cove saluted and ran toward a group of waiting soldiers, while Lander turned to gaze at the snow-covered camp. There were hundreds of hovels crammed against a rock wall riddled with caves. They were positioned due north of the westernmost point of Grimble Island and east of the dragons' mountain fortresses. It was as defensible a camp as they could find but never intended as more than a temporary home. They usually called it a camp and many still called it after the scout who discovered an old crossing here. Lener Spry had led the team who found the camp, and the official name was Lener's Crossroads. Lander watched the falling snow. *Will we ever find our true home?*

"Yer Highness-ness?"

Lander spun around and found Nickel Drekker, who waved his hand in a nonchalant flourish instead of bowing.

"Oh, hello there, Nickel. Are you coming in your sister's stead? I ordered her to report."

"Aye, that," Nickel replied. "I've indeed a message off me sister. Shall I give it to ye guts-and-all or shall I smooth the fur a bit?"

"Guts-and-all, if you please."

"Aye. She says, 'Tell that Lander Lordling that I'll come report to hisself when I've did the thing hisself asked me t'do first. I can't do as he asked and set these many kidlings up to an entirely new life here with their old enemies and be reporting to hisself every five minutes.' So said she to report t'ye, and having done did it, I'll be off." Nickel started walking away.

"Hold on," Lander replied. "Tell her..." he paused, shook his head, and continued. "Tell her she's doing well. Tell her to keep up the good work."

Nickel nodded, eyes wide. "She needs very little encouragement, that one. Winnie's been as headstrong as a neck wrestler all her days."

Lander nodded. "Ask her to report to me when she is free."

"Aye, Highness," he said, and he sauntered off toward the Drekker hold.

Lander watched him go, his mind full of concern for the young buck—for all the young bucks and does. *Will they have a chance at life?*

Prince Lander & the Dragon War

The camp felt ominously empty at present, with most of the little ones and their mothers hidden away in the caves. It felt bereft of life. He thought of his younger brother Davis, who had been killed by the cunning of the murderous King Namoz. Davis had died defending this place and its inhabitants. Would Lander soon do the same? *Will we all?*

Hurried footfalls, and Lander spun. He knew the meaning behind every kind of step in this snow and in every other condition, having been in an almost constant state of war his whole life. That sound meant news from his father.

The messenger stepped forward and bowed. His breath hung white in the icy air. Gasping for breath, he stammered, "Your Majesty—beg pardon, I mean, Your Highness." He coughed.

"Take your time, son," Lander said.

"Thank you, sir," he replied, hands on his hips as he inhaled deeply. "Your father, sir, says that there's no sign of them beasts out east."

"Thank you," Lander said. "Now, get something warm in you, son."

The messenger bowed and walked off toward the provisions tent where a big black pot steamed overtop a fire.

Captain Cove jogged over. "Sir," he said, bowing neatly, "no word from Prince Grant yet."

Lander grimaced. "There wouldn't be if they've been overwhelmed. Father's messenger said there's nothing out east. So either Father was wrong or it was just a scouting party."

Brindle peered into the forest over the west ridge. "If it's scouts, then they'll slink back again, and no trouble done."

"*If.*"

"Aye."

Lander motioned toward the provisioner's fire. "Let's get warmed up while we wait, Captain."

"Aye, sir."

They walked toward the fire, where the messenger was holding forth to the gathered band of soldiers and support staff. Lander smiled as the buck, tongue-tied just moments before, was now speaking with exaggerated gestures while his audience shook their heads.

"He's certainly found his tongue," Lander said as they drew nearer.

"Sir, I fear..." Brindle began, but the messenger buck's words were now audible.

Prince Lander & the Dragon War

"...and the old codger sends five teams—five!—to the place the enemy ain't even been. I told the bucks he'd get us all killed or else we'd be wandering east and never come back. I was afraid he'd send me the wrong way with a message, seeing that he don't know east from west!" There was laughter and nodding heads until the bucks surrounding the messenger began to notice the coming prince.

Coughs. Nods. Wide eyes. But the messenger, whose back was turned to Lander and Captain Cove, went on. "And he's sent only two teams west—the senile old geezer—and Prince Grant'll like as not be killed by his folly. He's sent him to face the dragons with less forces than he takes himself the wrong way? He'll get Prince Grant killed, sure enough. Prince Lander'd never do that. We've no chance unless we've got Lander as king—" He spun around, finally aware that something was wrong.

Prince Lander glowered at the young soldier, and an anguished silence settled over the gathered bucks. Lander pointed at the messenger. "Clap that traitor in irons!"

"Aye, sir," Captain Cove said, and he crossed

to the buck and gripped him roughly by both arms from behind. Some of those gathered seemed ready to lunge at Captain Cove and tear their comrade free.

Lander eyed the others coldly. "All of you could hang for this. Every one of you. None of you would be here were it not for King Whitson. He deserves better than this ungrateful treason. I am ashamed of you all." He turned and walked swiftly away.

The angry messenger's voice stopped him. "I've only said what we've all been thinking, sir. We want you to lead us, Your Majesty!"

Lander spun back, seething. "Don't call me that! I am not the king. You're a traitor—like Grimble himself— and might as well be allied to the dragons." A crowd was gathering now, rabbits from all around camp drawn by the commotion around the provisioner's tent.

The messenger writhed in Captain Cove's grip. "We'll all die if he goes on! We need *you* as our king!"

Captain Cove pulled him back. "Silence, you!"

Lander stood in an open space amid the camp, facing a growing crowd of unsettled angry young bucks. He glowered at the messenger. "Another word, soldier, and there will be no way back for you. This is a capital crime."

Another voice came from the crowd. "Whitson Codger will kill us all!" Lander couldn't see who said it. Another shouted, "Lander is our king!"

"No," Lander snapped. "No!"

"If not him, Prince Grant or Lemual, then!" another shouted.

The noise grew, and the bucks were emboldened by their growing numbers as more gathered. Captain Cove dragged the messenger away, and Lander heard a noise of crunching snow and shouts from behind.

Lander turned back to see a band of bucks carrying the limp form of a rabbit into the camp.

His heart sank. One of the bucks broke loose and ran ahead. Panicked and gasping, he reached Lander as the crowd of bucks gathered around them.

"It's Prince Grant, Your Highness," he said between heaving breaths as he scrubbed at his eyes. "Your Highness, the dragons got him."

Chapter Eight

"He's not dead yet," the field medic said as Lander reached his brother.

Prince Grant was wounded badly, his head wrapped in a makeshift bandage that seeped scarlet.

Lander knelt by his brother. "Hold on, Grant. We're going to get you fixed up." He lurched up, shouting orders, and got the train moving again.

"Where to, sir?" the medic asked.

"My father's quarters," Lander replied, then shouted, "Send for Doctor Grimes! Ask her to meet us in the king's quarters."

"Aye, sir!" one of Grant's loyal bucks called, and he darted off. Lander saw that he, too, was bleeding. In fact, they were all wounded. And they were fewer than when they set out.

"Help these soldiers," Lander shouted, and he moved closer to examine their wounds. Four of them carried Grant tenderly. Lander laid his hand on the nearest one's shoulder. "Now, bucks, let some fresh fellows carry the prince."

Others stepped close and reached for the prince, but the bearers only glared up at them. It was clear they intended to see their captain to his bed. Lander nodded to the soldiers who had stepped up, and they backed off, saluting as they did. Worry showed on every face. No matter how unpopular the king might be with some young bucks at present, Prince Grant clearly had their respect.

That made sense. Grant could be impatient and rash and always leaned toward action instead of overthinking.

As they drew closer to the king's quarters, Doctor Grimes and Mother met them at the entrance. The doctor made a quick assessment, then pointed inside. "Hurry," she said.

Outside, soldiers knelt with heads down. Lander paused to look at them, ordered the rushing medics to attend to the wounded, then darted inside.

Prince Lander & the Dragon War

Hurrying to the back room, Lander saw doctors and nurses urgently working on his brother. Grant wasn't moving. Lander crossed to his brother's side, knelt by the bed, and took his limp hand. Doctor Grimes caught Lander's eye, and he read her expression quickly. *She needs room to work.* Rising, he helped clear a space around the bed for her, pulling others back and leading them into the front room. With a last glance at Grant's apparently lifeless face, he left the room. Mother came to him, and he embraced her. Queen Lillie wept quietly.

"He is in good hands," Lander whispered, still dazed by this blow. He had seen much injury and death in his years at war, but never Grant, whom he loved so deeply. He wasn't sure he could bear to lose another brother—his youngest brother. "Doctor Grimes will save him if…"

They both knew what he didn't say. *If he can be saved.*

* * *

They waited in the front room of the king's quarters for half an hour, leaving the back room to Doctor Grimes and her staff. From time to time they heard shouts and cries from the camp outside, and Lander almost left to discover what the noise meant. But he stayed, believing his place was with Mother as they awaited news. He knew if anything was urgent outside, one of the captains would come for him. Finally, the door opened, and King Whitson entered, flanked by Prince Lemual, who looked small beside Father. The king's face was grave. "What news?" he asked, reaching for Mother's hands.

She tried to speak but couldn't and collapsed into his arms. He looked to Lander.

"We don't know, Father. We've been letting Doctor Grimes work. Perhaps it's a good thing she hasn't come to us with an update. We haven't asked."

"That is well."

They sat there, the bewildered family, for a long time. No one spoke, but they held hands and by many small signs showed their affection for one another through their grief.

After some time the door opened again, and Captain Walters entered. "Your Majesty," he said, bowing.

"Captain?" Whitson asked, concern etched on

his haggard face.

"Sir, we have a bit of a problem outside."

Lander stepped forward. "Shall I deal with it, Father?"

Captain Walters nodded. "It might be better if the prince sees to it, sir."

King Whitson scowled, anger briefly flashing on his face. Then he inhaled deeply, nodded, and sat down by Mother. Lander bowed to his parents, then followed Captain Walters to the door.

Walters stopped at the door and whispered. "Sir, they are angry—the young bucks, especially. They love Prince Grant and have heard him question the king sometimes, so they think he has the right ideas. They think the king has killed Prince Grant by his madness—by sending him where the dragons were spotted without the proper reinforcements. I think they believe the king was eliminating a rival. They are near rioting."

"I understand," Lander replied and opened the door.

It was a sickening sight. The king's guards were lined up and squared off against a band of rowdy young soldiers, all glaring at the king's quarters in fury. Troubled officers stood in the middle distance, some with hands on sword hilts.

Silence settled when they saw Lander emerge. Then a shout came from among the young bucks. "Has the feeble old king killed our Prince Grant?"

A few bucks murmured approval of the question while others, officers among the guard, snapped back at them to be quiet.

Lander held up a hand for silence. When they complied, he hung his head. This was sad, but an anger rose in him toward the young malcontents that he could barely contain. His mind told him they might have reasonable concerns, but his heart told him they deserved to be executed for treason.

"Will you put forth a leader to speak for you?" Lander asked through gritted teeth.

A chorus of complaints rose from the group, and Lander quickly understood that they believed the buck would be arrested for treason. He held up his hand again. "No, I guarantee him safety. I guarantee him freedom to speak and return to you unharmed. Have I ever lied to you? I give you my word."

They talked among themselves, and after a few arguments and shoves were given and received, a tall white-furred buck walked forward. Lander knew him. This was Filmun, Guard Derk's oldest son. His father was an old, faithful soldier—one who'd bled with Whitson many times. In fact, Derk was there on the guard line, his pike in hand and his face set in a shocked, pained expression. *He has the face of one who feels betrayed. Maybe I have it, too.*

At Captain Walters' command, the guards parted to let Filmun approach Prince Lander. As the buck approached, Lander drew his sword. Filmun stopped, flinching back as angry howls sounded from the disgruntled bucks.

Lander wanted to bring his blade around and do his worst to Filmun, then start into the others. But he slowly raised it high and cast it on the ground. The angry bucks quieted, and Filmun walked forward again, drawing his own blade and tossing it to lie near the prince's.

"Now we are equal," Filmun said, smiling wryly.

Lander gazed at Filmun through squinted eyes, head cocked sideways. He said nothing. The young buck drew closer, slowing as he neared the prince. It would be usual to bow, and Lander let the youth live with the discomfort.

S. D. Smith

He did bow slightly, eventually, and the angry bucks groaned behind him. Still, Lander didn't move or speak. Filmun fidgeted, glancing from the crowd to the prince and back.

Finally, Filmun couldn't wait any longer, and he opened his mouth to speak. That's when Lander spoke loud and clear. "Filmun Derkson. Why?"

Filmun was unbalanced by Lander's direct words, and he stepped back. He seemed to receive the question as a blow. "Why? Well, we've been led by your father into dangers, and we think that, we believe, we need new leadership. The bucks want a new king."

"You want Whitson Mariner, savior of our community and kind, the buck who brought us here from the ruin of Golden Coast, to die?"

"Not that, sir, no—"

"You want to kill King Whitson Mariner?"

"I didn't say that!" Filmun cried.

"Then what do you want?" Lander snapped.

Filmun inhaled deeply and shouted back. "We want him to abdicate and let you, or one of your brothers, rule instead, sir! He's not fit to command!"

The crowd shouted agreement, and the guards pressed closer, pikes raised. "Hear him!" the young bucks cried, rattling their weapons and slapping their thighs.

Lander winced. "What if we asked your fathers?"

Filmun glanced at his father, saw that pained expression on his face, and then back at the prince.

He swallowed hard, then raised his voice above the crowd. "The king will kill us all, just as he's killed Prince Grant!"

Lander was outraged, but he worked hard to control himself. He saw his own internal battle being played out in the guards, officers, and young bucks who stepped and scowled and seemed agitated to the point of blows. This was a simmering soup on the verge of boiling over.

Filmun stepped closer, and Lander leaned in to listen. Filmun whispered, "They have been talking all this time, sir. I know it's not the best way, what we've done. But it just happened. It's been brewing for a long time. I know these ones, sir. I'm not the most enraged. They sent me forward because they know I'm reasonable and can negotiate. They are content with that for now."

"And what if that doesn't work?" Lander asked, more alarmed by this whispering than all the shouting that had gone before.

"Your Highness," Filmun said, "if Prince Grant is dead, then they will revolt. There will be blood in our camp, and they won't stop until we have a new king."

Lander's anger swelled, but he nodded and

stepped back, crossing his arms and pulling at the fur of his chin. His Father's words from earlier echoed in his mind. *I don't know what to do.*

Just then, a scream came from inside the king's quarters, followed by a cry of "Nooooo!"

Lander spun around. That was his mother's cry. He knew it.

They all knew it.

Chapter Nine

The crowd of angry youths cried out, and the guards aimed their pikes. A clash was imminent. Filmun dashed back to the young bucks.

Lander's head swam, and his heart sank. *I have lost my brother. And we will see a civil war.*

A hurried conference was held among the young soldiers. Quick agreement followed, and their determined faces swiveled to the thin line of guards that stood between them and the royal family. They stepped forward, drawing swords and aiming arrows.

"Hold, there!" came a cry of such authority that the raucous camp settled and turned to gaze on King Whitson Mariner himself, newly emerged from the open doorway. Captain Walters stood just over his left shoulder and had clearly informed the king of what was happening.

Lander stood alone in the acrid space between the brewing battle and the weary old king.

King Whitson raised his hand. His face was haggard and worried, and he seemed to be struggling in his mind to find the right words. Just as he began to speak, another form appeared in the doorway.

Grant!

A gasp came from the crowd as the injured young prince hobbled into view.

"He's alive!" someone in the crowd shouted, and a murmur of delight and confusion rippled through the anxious camp.

Lander raced to his badly wounded brother and reached out to help prop him up. Grant shook his head. "They must see me standing alone," he whispered hoarsely.

Lander wavered between insisting on helping his brother and allowing him to complete his task. He stepped back slowly. "I'm here if you need me."

The camp quieted now, and Grant raised his cracking voice to be heard by all who were near enough. "I have always told the truth as I see it,

Prince Lander & the Dragon War

have I not? I don't often hold back. I am one for action and impatient of delay. I have been sometimes accused of being over-honest." Some uneasy laughter. Heads nodding. Grant continued. "You believe my father was wrong for sending only two teams to where the dragons were spotted. You think him wrong for taking more forces to the opposite ridge?" More head nodding, some murmurs of affirmation. "Well, what you may not have thought of is that the dragons spotted on the west ridge were—by the full agreement of the king, his military councilors, and his sons—almost certainly either a scouting party or a ruse to bait us into a conflict on that side while they attack from the rear. You see, my father—King Whitson—has been planning for the final defense of this camp for many years. He has not made a rash and foolish decision in the moment. No. He has followed a protocol decided upon long ago, adapting it nimbly to the information available. He has done what the best military leaders in our midst have agreed to do." Grant's voice was weakening, and Lander fought back an urge to help his brother stand steady. But Grant squinted against the pain and continued. "I was hurt because I

engaged the dragon scouts—against my father's orders—and I endangered not only myself but those loyal and brave bucks under my command. What you see as the king's folly and my harm was really the opposite. Forgive me, Father, I beg. And forgive me, friends," he said, extending a shaking hand toward the angry young bucks, "for this foolish...this foolish—" His eyes rolled back, and he pitched forward. Lander lunged to catch him.

Chapter Ten

An uneasy day passed as Prince Grant lay near death. The whole camp waited on edge as unspoken or whispered divisions formed fault lines that threatened to break all apart.

Lander stood by his father as the king announced a blanket pardon for every buck who raised their voices or arms against him. Lander had hoped Father would only pardon the malcontents on the condition that they swore a new fealty oath. But the old king said that traitors don't keep those oaths anyway. It would only mask the problem and intensify the rage of the most violent ones.

More days passed as the army prepared for an attack, and each evening Lander, exhausted and discouraged, stumbled into his father's house to see his brother only just clinging to life. Most mornings he came to visit too. And this morning, he aimed to get answers.

"Be honest with me, Doctor Grimes," Lander asked, "do you think Grant will live?"

Doctor Grimes glanced around and lowered her voice. "I'm sorry to say I do not. But Prince Grant is stubborn, and it wouldn't be the first time he went against expectations."

Lander nodded gravely. "Fight back, Grant," he whispered. "I need you."

"I'll leave you," Doctor Grimes said, bowing as she turned. Lander noticed that Lemual was waiting a few yards away, polite enough not to interrupt but close enough to hear.

"Doctor," Lander said, taking Father's memory tonic from the nightstand, "would this help Grant? I have heard you say how powerful it is for the mind. Maybe it could help him?"

Doctor Grimes reached for the tonic and replaced it on the bedside table. "No, never, Your Highness. That is mostly poison. It is strong, and it would kill anyone who takes it."

Lander frowned. "I have seen Father take it hundreds of times."

"Yes, he must have it for his condition. But he also takes a weekly concoction containing the principal antidote to the negative effects of the tincture. Without it, he would die."

"Without the antidote he would die?" Lander whispered, appalled. "How long would it take?"

"Around ten days, the last few being more wretched than you can imagine."

"We must not let this become known," Lander said. "There are too many who wish for Father's death."

"I agree. It's only your mother and now you—and Prince Lemual, there listening near us—who know about the antidote."

"Thank you, Doctor, for caring for Father all these years. And now for Grant, too."

"It is my great honor to serve your family, Your Highness," she said, bowing low. She turned and walked away.

Prince Lemual passed the doctor and hurried to Grant's bedside. He looked with deep concern at his brother, then over at Lander. Lander smiled sadly, answering the question he knew Lemual wanted to ask. "The same. He's on the edge of going."

A thin tear slipped from the corner of Lemual's eye. "He will claw his way back from the edge." He snorted and wiped at his nose and eyes. "That's what Grant does. He fights. Come on, Grant, fight! Fight like never before. Fight to keep on fighting."

Lander wiped his own eyes and watched silently for a while.

After a time, Lander rose and stretched. "Let's take a walk, Lem."

Lemual nodded, rose slowly, and, with one last sad glance at Grant, followed Lander out.

Lander limped along as they passed the nurses stationed in the next room, then followed the hall to the doorway, which was opened for them by a thin guard. Both princes pulled their scarves tighter against the wind, which blew thickening snowflakes in a swirl around the camp. Soldiers gathered beside the building, leaning into fires and trying to talk loudly enough to be heard over the wind. Saluting, Lander passed the first sentries outside, as he led Lemual along the winding route south toward the heart of the camp. They passed more soldiers at their posts, many shivering. Lander felt his leg grow numb in the cold. He hoped he didn't have to run anytime soon.

Finally, they came to a well-guarded gate. Past the gate, down a winding path, rose the high rock formation against which the entire camp was positioned.

"When's your relief, Dawson?" Lander asked a shivering red rabbit.

"An hour hence, Your Highness," Dawson replied, bowing.

"Thank you for protecting this gate, Dawson. You know what it means, I dare say?"

"I know if the enemy gets past us here, then it's a free shot to the most vulnerable in this community. And I won't have that, sir." He shook his head, and the others joined in. Lander noticed that a few of the guards at this gate had been among the vocal band of young agitators. He nodded coolly toward them. They bowed briefly, then looked away.

"My..." Lander began but stopped. He had been about to give them a history lesson centered on all his father had done for the widows—the old ones, with them for so many years, and the new ones created by their valiant defensive battles—and all the orphans and younglings in their midst. Instead, he only shook his head. "Thank you, bucks, each and every one of you, for your service. We must all do our part to defend this community."

"Aye, sir," Dawson replied. "May I ask how your brother, the prince, fares?"

"The same." Lander winced, nodded again to the bucks, and walked on.

Lemual sighed. "I thought for sure there was a stern lecture brewing for those bucks back there. I feared for them."

Lander smiled. "They have only just barely been spared."

"Them, but not me?" Lemual asked.

Lander nodded. "You are wise, Lem. A good trait for a king."

Lemual shook his head. "It won't come to that."

"It probably will." Lander reached out and laid his hand gently on Lemual's head. "I'm sorry to say it, but Grant probably wouldn't live even if we weren't about to be wiped out by the combined dragon and Grimble armies. But we are."

"I can't leave, Lander," Lemual said, a little louder than Lander expected. They both glanced back down the trail to the guards. They looked on, some shivering.

Lander rubbed at his eyes. "I'm not asking you to leave now. That's not the plan. But if things go as they could and the worst happens, you will have to take the Third Scouts and go. You will have to do your duty and help preserve our kind."

Lemual shook his head, frowning. "I don't—"

"I know, Lem. I know. But you know the Third Scouts unit was formed for that purpose. Bucks and does, all around your age, able to go out in the wilderness and keep going. You may have to."

Lemual turned back and gazed toward the soldiers at the gate. "I know I'm small, and some say I can't fight like you or Grant. Maybe they're right. In fact, they are. But I can help. I'm so keen to help, Lander. I can't leave. I'd rather die in battle, like Davis."

"We don't always get to decide what our role is," Lander said, moving his hand to Lemual's shoulder. "Our duty may be a pleasure, but our duty isn't just to find pleasure."

Lemual turned and smiled. "Is that Father speaking through you once again, my tall handsome elder and most faithful brother?"

Lander grinned back. "That one was from another father to me, Lord Fleck Blackstar. I wish you could have known him."

"A hero who stayed and fought," Lemual said, his frown returning.

"A hero who knew his duty."

"I only want to keep the old oath myself, Lander. My place beside you. My blood for yours. Till the Green Ember rises," and Lemual patted the lump of Lander's shirt where the emerald gem hung on Lander's chest from a stout chain, "or the end of the world."

Lander reached inside his shirt and produced the emerald. The Green Ember. It was a symbol of his future right to rule—right and duty to rule. He was the heir. Their father bore the Ruling Stone, a ruby gem worn by the sovereign. Lander gazed at the emerald. "Lem, if the end of the world comes, then you'll go on with the Third Scouts. That is Father's wish, and mine."

"Father's wishes have always been yours, Lander," Lemual said. "You're a faithful son, even when it's hard. And you've been a good big brother to me and Grant."

"I love you, Lem," Lander replied. "I'll love you to the end—to the end of the world."

Chapter Eleven

Lander and Lemual walked to the edge of the cave wall, then ducked inside through the thin opening into a torchlit cave where seven archers stood ready. The archers bowed, then gave way, revealing a passage behind them. Lander led on, taking one of the torches from the wall as he went.

The cave tunnel, wide in places and frighteningly narrow in others, led past many openings into wider rooms. Inside were cozy, warm quarters walled off by hung curtains that seemed to glow in various colors over their entrances. The two brothers walked on, eventually coming to a secluded cave at the end of a long passage.

There was no curtain on this entrance, and firelight played along the opening. Lander and

Lemual eased closer and looked inside. The room was small and held shelves of books broken up by odd relics and other ancient decor. A stone sword, old and crusted over, was mounted on a wall. Lander spotted a table near another wall where several different-sized pots held measured doses of substances ground by mortar and pestle. Herbs and dried-up plants were piled in neat boxes. A thin twist of smoke rose from the single candle on that table. Someone had been working there recently. In the middle of the room, two forms sat at a desk. One was bent over, thin and aged. The other was young and as healthy as a rabbit could be. The young doe was speaking.

The older doe bent her head and raised her hand, ending the younger rabbit's flow of words. "Come in, Your Highnesses," Mother Saramack said.

The princes walked in, and Lander locked eyes with Mother Saramack's guest. *Hollie Grimble*. Anger flared inside him. Until now, he hadn't even introduced Lem to this secret repository of their inheritance, to this treasure room of mysteries and sacred trusts. And Hollie Grimble—*Grimble!*—was admitted? "What is she doing here?" he snapped. Hollie's mouth bent in an angry frown, touched with embarrassment.

Mother Saramack was slowly getting up from her chair, with Hollie's help. She bent even further than her frame already bent and bowed. "Your Highnesses."

Lander crossed quickly and reached for her, helping her slowly back into her chair. "Mother Saramack, please don't take the trouble of all that. I'd rather bow to you."

"No, my prince," she replied, easing into the chair again. "You must be what you are and let me be who I am."

"Who you are," Lander replied, "is one of our greatest treasures, and I shouldn't have snapped at you. Please forgive me?"

"Of course, my dear Prince Lander," she replied. "Hollie is our enemy's oldest child, and it's not odd that you would question her presence."

Hollie had been seething since Lander's harsh demand. She rose. "I don't need your permission to go where I wish, princeling!"

Mother Saramack cocked her head and laughed. "Actually, you do, Hollie Grimble. If you are one of us, one of our camp and community, then that is exactly what the prince does. He leads. And he has done it ever so well. He leads with kindness and cunning. You would be wise to listen to him."

Hollie's head hung low. She shook it, then looked up. "You're right, Mother Saramack, of course. And I owe you more than obedience, Prince Lander. I owe you my life, and the lives of all the Grimble younglings. How is your leg, sir?"

Lander bowed neatly. "I must apologize for my rudeness at seeing you here. I am...defensive...of this place and this honored person, but I was wrong to be so unkind. My leg is much better, and I thank you for asking."

"Hollie," Mother Saramack said, "this is Prince Lemual. Prince Lemual, this is your sworn enemy's eldest child, Hollie."

Lemual bowed. "I'm very pleased to meet you."

"The honor is mine," Hollie said.

Lemual smiled as Lander frowned. Then, seeing one another, the brothers' expressions quickly shifted so that the reverse was true. Hollie looked at her feet, one stepping on the other. Lander coughed. Lemual smoothed his tunic, then pulled at a loose thread.

Mother Saramack grinned at them. "I love an awkward moment. You get so few truly, deeply, magnificently awkward moments in life. And we've just had one. I hope you savored it as much as I."

Lander grinned. "You never disappoint, Mother Saramack."

She smiled, then turned to Hollie. "You may go, my dear. See the votary down the tunnel about the lines for memory—the prester is ill, I think—and then see the provisioner for fresh supplies for my table. And remember this, my precious doe: you have value beyond your ability to save and serve others. What's in your blood is not the certain omen of your future."

Hollie hugged the old doe, then bowed quickly to the princes and left.

Lander watched her go, then turned back to Mother Saramack. There were tears in her eyes.

"Why these tears, Mother?" Lander asked.

Mother Saramack smiled sadly, then gazed into the dark far corner of the room. "She has a hard road, that one. A very long, very hard, road. But in the end, there will be a golden home."

Lander bowed his head. He had heard Mother Saramack say many strange things in his time, and he could identify with the oddness. There were times when he, too, would seem to see beyond what was present, into another kind of seeing. About his own episodes and hers, he usually remained silent. He had learned to let them be and not ask too many questions of Mother Saramack. She usually didn't know the answers anyway and seemed annoyed that anyone would ask. He did ask a question, but not about her words regarding Hollie Grimble. "Mother, are you feeling well?"

"I decline, sir," she replied. "Indeed, I do." She glanced at the table with the pots, then back at Lander. "I have made certain decisions that allow me to be free to decline. I will not be needed here much longer, and I have trained my replacements."

"It must take many, indeed," Lemual said reverently, "to dare try to replace you. It would take an army of wise and generous rabbits."

"Your Highness is very kind. You are short of stature but not in manners," she replied. "However, you have not come to speak of me. You have troubles of your own. Questions, I dare to guess?"

Lemual said, "Is that old stone blade Flint's sword? It doesn't look very deadly."

"No, Highness," she replied. Lander smiled.

Prince Lander & the Dragon War

He had made the same assumption as a young buck. Mother Saramack continued. "That is an old sword that has been important to royals for many years. It has its own history but serves now as a kind of decoy to the real thing."

Lander stepped closer. "Mother Saramack, I do want to ask you about the real sword. You have been studying the problem of Father's sword, I know. I'm grateful for that, and I hope you discover something to help us. I know you have been deep in your research and in working with your apprentices, so you won't know about the problems in the camp."

Mother Saramack laughed softly. "You mean the problem that nearly half the soldiers are young and foolish and are against your father?"

Lander held up his hands. "It's not possible for you to miss something significant, is it?"

"I have my ears tuned to trouble," she said. "Those loyal to the king number roughly the same as the fools?"

"I believe so. More, of course, if we include wives and families. Most of the young and angry band are unmarried bucks."

"Yes," Mother Saramack said, her hands

meeting in a peak of fingers that she set against her lips in concentration. "The question then becomes 'Who is in the middle?'"

"The middle?" Lemual asked. "I don't understand."

Mother Saramack looked up at the brothers. "For instance, where do the Drekkers stand in all this?"

"The Drekkers?" Lander frowned. "I don't know. Some of them are helping with resettling the Grimble faction children, but otherwise I couldn't say. Who ever knows what the Drekkers are thinking?"

"Precisely," Mother Saramack said. "Perhaps if we did, we would be able to tip the balance against the young fools."

Lander nodded, understanding dawning. "I see. Yes. But, Mother, it's impossible to figure out what they're thinking."

"Have you tried?"

"No. No, I haven't."

"Has your father tried?"

Lander shook his head. "I don't think so."

"No, he hasn't," she said. "And no king or prince in a long time has done anything other than either hold the Drekkers in contempt or see them as an odd joke. At best they are seen as useful. Maybe it's time that changed."

Lander considered the urgency of their situation. The crisis in the camp and the impending invasion. "Do I have time?"

Mother Saramack shrugged. "Do you have time to do anything else?"

Lemual stroked his chin. "There are other groups, perhaps none as large as the Drekkers, who are outsiders. The Halvers, the Goldites—even the Chelms. We could go to them all. It would shore up our coalition."

Mother Saramack nodded. "It would, sure. But time is pressing, and the Drekkers are the key. They have taken in several of the outsider clans, and most of the others have close ties to them. Carry the Drekkers, and you carry the camp."

"Yes, Mother," Lander said. "Thank you. As ever, you have given us the gift of your wisdom."

She smiled, then frowned. "I wish I could unlock the secret of the starsword, dear princes, but it eludes me. To my intense frustration, I cannot find the missing part of the mystery. The kings have buried—possibly for good reason—both the sword and the secrets, and their sages have not extended the cord of its meaning down the long line of the wise. A heedless folly for the ages. Indeed, I fairly rage at them within my frail old being. But my anger is not profitable. Recovery is all. If you will excuse me, my royal bucks, I shall resume the hunt."

"May you find what you seek," Lander said. "For all our sakes."

Mother Saramack nodded and, squinting, whispered, "Flint's sword is wrapped up in our destiny in ways of which I can only glimpse dimly at the edges. It must be buried. It must be used. It must not be used. It must not be kept. It must be broken. All these are true, but I can't say how, for they contradict."

"A paradox," Lemual said.

Mother Saramack inhaled deeply. "A conundrum with the weight of destiny pressed upon it."

Chapter Twelve

Lander led his brother away from the cave wall, out past the gate with its shivering soldiers, and through the camp toward the northeast corner.

"What will you do when the war's over, Lander?" Lemual asked.

"Assuming we win and we're both still alive, somehow?"

"Preferably."

"I haven't thought about it much. Mother always talked about making cider. We did one year, before you came along. It was amazing."

"You'd make cider?"

Lander laughed. "Yeah, I'd make cider. And we'd drink it together and tell stories about the war."

Lemual nodded. "The war we won and didn't die in."

"That one, yes."

"Okay, we'll drink together then, brother. But maybe you should get married and have a family."

"I hope to, Lem. I really do."

They walked on in silence a while, thinking of that distant taste of cider.

There was no official separation of different bands in the camp, but the northeast corner had really become the Drekkers' hold. They didn't have their own sentries, officially, but they had strong bucks who just happened to walk the perimeters in a regular pattern. One burly buck stopped his walking and stood between the princes at what was a kind of gateway into the hold. This opening was surrounded by carts lined up to edge the perimeter of their camp within a camp.

Anger flared inside Lander. *I don't have time for these games.* He breathed deeply, trying to calm himself. *But this is why I'm here. Because it matters.* He smiled at the sentry. "Good day, soldier."

"Highness," he replied with a voice that was almost a sneer. His apathetic bow and smirking eyes gave a clear message to the prince. *You have*

Prince Lander & the Dragon War

little authority within this hold.

"I come to visit Chief Heckle," Lander said.

The guard frowned, then shook his head. "Chief's at the match—wouldn't be free and back to parley till eventide at earliest." Another unofficial sentry joined the first, and soon a small crowd of strong guards barred the gateway to the hold.

Lander bit his lip. *Curse their games!* The Drekkers had several sports that they took very seriously. Most were rough games that often led to significant injuries—even deaths, occasionally. At one point Whitson had attempted to ban the games because they threatened the readiness of the army. But it only led to the Drekkers never speaking of the games outside their hold again, and the king, distracted by other matters and frustrated by a lack of cooperation from the Drekker leaders, let the demand go. This pattern of decree from the royals followed by deeper entrenchment on the part of the Drekkers was the very problem Mother Saramack had identified. *I don't have time for these games or those games!* Lander breathed deeply again, casting an angry sidelong glance over at Lemual. He looked up at the sentry. "Who's playing?"

The first guard looked down. "Uh," he stuttered,

seeming to remember the kerfuffle surrounding the banning of the games, "Uh, it's a..."

Another of the Drekker bucks, one newly arrived and as thick as the two princes combined, flourished a toothless grin and spoke up. "Agh, Doove, ye ought to know, it's yer own cousin's clanside match. Yer Princeships," he went on, shaking his head at Doove, "forgive ye my pal's sudden density. The match's between Gates Hale Raiders and Tane-side Chippers. I'm for the Chips, but Doove's for Gates Hale. They'll be walloped, I assure ye," he said, wagging a finger at Doove, who groaned and rolled his eyes.

"Thanks, good soldier," Lander said. "Your name?"

The thick Drekker nodded in a kind of happy head-wag. "Name's Pusher. Biggting Pusher. Me da's a Pusher, too, if ye can believe it. Followed his work all the way on. Pushing like a good'n. Yer Royalships need anything pushed right about now? I'm free and off me pushing work for the even', and I'm near-enough killed off sentry duty too." Again, a groan emerged from Doove and the rest. "But I'd happily push anything you'd like. Just point and say push!" He cackled and mimed pointing, then pushing. "Me da always says that, and it gets me every time. 'Just point and say push,' says he, and we all break up laughing like eejits."

Doove shook his head and moaned. "Exactly like eejits."

"As a matter of fact, there *is* something I need pushed right about now," Lander said, "just beside where they're playing the match."

"Well, foller me, Prince Marinerson," Biggting Pusher said, hooking his thick arm toward the hold. "I'll show ye. I can push like a kidling loose on Hesterfest in the rain."

Lander followed the hulking buck into the hold, Lemual close beside him and the befuddled sentries left behind. "Now, Biggting," Lander said, "are you close to the chief?"

"Well," Biggting replied, scratching his ear, "I'm not rightly erllowed near hisself, on account of a mistake one er the other of us made—not sure if 'twas his'n or my'n—but other'n that proximity ban, ye could say I'm pretty close t'him."

They followed Biggting past little knots of thatch-topped huts built together in sets of six to ten. Snow-covered lanes wound around them, and they followed Biggting on as he walked in great strides, head held high—a bit too high to see the path well, for he tripped often. The village in the hold was mostly abandoned, though occasional rings of smoke curled out from the central chimney in a cluster of huts. After a short distance, they heard the sound of a crowd, rising and falling with excitement and fear. They walked through a portion of forest, and the trail rose into a hill dense with trees. Lander hadn't been here since they first settled this camp. Gasps followed cheers, and Lander smiled to hear the collective swell of expectation. Father sometimes spoke of the sports their community had played on Golden Coast. Sadly, they hadn't had much time to adopt them here in Natalia—not the big, organized ones. But the Drekkers had made time for it, even amid the hardships of war and wandering. Perhaps that was one of the things that kept them so close as a clan.

Soon they topped the rise and looked down on a clearing. Lander was glad to rest his sore leg, and he rubbed around the wound, then looked up again. They gazed down on a great oval, lined on the outside with tightly packed rabbits, all eagerly watching the action on the snowy field.

Prince Lander & the Dragon War

The players were locked in what looked like a fight, with some blocking and pushing and others kicking and tackling. Others dove in a pile, while teammates tried to tear their opponents off the stacked jumble of bodies. Lander glanced at Lemual. His eyes were wide with wonder. A brass cymbal crashed, and the players stopped their exertions, unpiled from the clump of bodies, and bumped heads gently and sportingly with their opponents. Then they crossed to opposite sides of the oval and sat.

Biggting clapped. "G'won, Chippies! That'll show 'em!"

"Who's winning?" Lemual asked.

"Rightly no idea," Biggting replied. "Foller me, My Royal Highnerz."

They followed him down the hill and toward the edge of the oval. There, surrounded by a formidable force of Drekkers, stood Chief Heckle.

The Drekkers stood blocking the entrance in a wide line, with crossed arms and rigid backs. No one bowed.

"Yer Highnesses," Chief Heckle said, "ye are not welcome here."

Chapter Thirteen

Lander stared at Chief Heckle, leader of the Drekkers, pondering what kind of response might be right. It would be easy to say something he'd later regret, pitching the balance of the army against his father. The Drekkers and other minor parties joining with the young fools—as Mother Saramack had called them—would be a disaster. Lander smiled, locking eyes with the Drekker leader. "That's disappointing, Chief Heckle. You are welcome at my table, my council, my court one day when I am king—may it not be soon. And I would be honored by, and grateful for, your presence."

Chief Heckle frowned, looking down. "This is a festival day, Prince Lander. We have kept this day to ourselves and only invited the rare outsider guest. That accounts, I hope ye will see, for my gruff greeting. Will ye walk with me?" The large buck, brown-furred with creeping streaks of grey all over, motioned to a path that ran around the outside of the oval.

Lander nodded and crossed to join the chief, trying to hide his limp. Lemual stepped toward Lander, his face showing concern. Lander turned back to meet his brother's gaze and plainly read his intent. *I don't trust them. I don't want you to go on alone.* Lander smiled and shook his head. *I'll be all right. This is important.* "Enjoy some sport, brother," he said aloud. "My bet's on the Chippers. I'll take a turn with our friend, Chief Heckle, and be back soon."

They walked away, and the chief reached out, taking hold of Lander's arm. At first this alarmed the prince, but he quickly remembered that this was a gesture of peace for the elders among the Drekkers. No one could be hurt as long as the elder was holding his arm, nor could any honest speech be held back. "This is the grip of truth, young prince," Chief Heckle said. "Do ye understand that?"

Prince Lander & the Dragon War

"Sir, my father raised me always to be in the grip of truth. I am and shall be honest."

"Honest? Yes, I believe ye. But ye might not say all. And our grip of truth means speaking even uncomfortable truths. For instance, that your brother Grant will likely die. That's a hard truth."

"It is," Lander answered. They walked on, the pain in Lander's leg intensifying.

"I know ye are having trouble with yer youths," Chief Heckle continued. "It's true of ours too, that they be as hot as a boiling kettle one moment and then as dumb as a stump the next. Take that youngster Biggting Pusher, for instance."

"But Chief," Lander replied, "he didn't seem hot-tempered at all."

The chief laughed and patted Lander's arm. "If yer looking for assurances of loyalty from us Drekkers and our wee coalition of outsiders-who-be-inside-for-now, ye are looking for the wrong thing. The Drekkers won't get involved like that. We'll decide our part when the crumbs have tumbled."

Lander's heart sank. "You'll wait for things to shake out, then decide if you're still in our coalition—still loyal to the king?"

"That's our way."

Lander reached out and gripped the chief's arm. "Your way's a coward's way."

"It may seem to be for such as ye," he replied. "But we Drekkers know our own story. It's not the same as yer ancestors. Ye weren't abandoned and left fer dead on the trek as we were those generations ago. Ye weren't doomed to roam fer ages in a barren wilderness, then to be lost and alone in the Mistenlands. Ye weren't forced to adapt and to band together when not nary one could see nor be seen. We made it through, then rejoined ye with reluctance on Golden Coast. Nor were we ever welcomed there as equals but set apart and set to work the labors ye didn't like. Always among us there are those who have growed up dreaming of being free of ye."

"Then why have you stayed with us—even through all of my father's journeys and wars? Why not go your way and be done with us?"

Chief Heckle nodded. "It'd be the easy thing, in many ways. But most of us remember our oldest oaths—oaths made by our eldest elders before the hard trekking, the bitter breaking, and the vexing reunion. The old oath to Flint and Fay and to their heirs forever."

Lander stopped. "And what of that old oath now? Why not keep it today and side with King Whitson Mariner, heir of Flint Firstking and savior of our kind?"

"The youths want another heir to reign—namely ye," Chief Heckle replied, squeezing

Lander's arm, "and ye are of Flint and Fay's line, are ye not?"

"My father lives," Lander growled.

"Aye, but is he—" the chief began, but he stopped when the crowd roared to life. "What scollywock is this?"

They turned and walked toward the oval, saw the crowd raising their fists and cheering loudly. "Isn't it just the resumption of the game?"

"No," Chief Heckle replied, "the game's only meant to carry on in an hour. Something's amiss."

They released one another and jogged toward the crowd, the chief shouting and shoving others aside so he and Lander could reach the inner ring and see the snow-covered field. Both bucks gazed open-mouthed at what they saw.

"Lemual!" Lander shouted.

Chief Heckle cursed. "That's another prince what'll be killed for certain."

Chapter Fourteen

Lander rushed onto the snowy field, where Lemual stood with a sling in his hand, facing off against a buck bigger and stronger even than Biggting Pusher. Bigger, stronger, and faster. The Drekker champion swung his sling and leapt in acrobatic flips. He was lined up across from the stationary prince.

"What are you doing, Lem?" Lander hissed, reaching his brother.

"Stand aside, Lander," Lemual replied coolly. "This scum challenged me. I'm doing this for Father's cause."

"Dying?" Lander said. "He already has one son on the edge of death on top of the one he already lost. You want to add a third?"

"You don't understand two things, big brother," Lemual said. "This villain insulted Father. He said he wouldn't follow his king if things came to a fight in the camp. And you also don't know—"

Lander cut him off. "That's enough. We're going."

"Ye can't bolt now, Highness."

Lander spun around to see Nickel Drekker approaching, his face concerned. Winnie was behind him. The twins scanned the crowd and then focused on the two princes. Lemual continued to stare across at the enormous, agile opponent.

Lander squinted back at the twins. "We can't leave? Whyever not? We're the king's sons!"

"Aye, ye are that," Nickel said, his face screwed up in concern. "But if ye do leave like that, after a challenge's been throwed out and accepted, then ye will leave all goodwill and honor behind ye, and ye'll throw away yer hopes of swaying the chief to yer side."

"We don't have a side!" Lander snapped. "We have the way—the right way!"

Winnie drew closer, nodding at first, then shaking her head. "Ye might be right, but Grimbles don't agree, nor do the Frustrated Band of

Prince Lander & the Dragon War

Hot Youngbloods. I don't say yer wrong, but I do say ye have convincing to do, here and elsewheres."

Nickel nodded. "Winnie's right, Highness. If ye leave, ye lose the Drekkers."

Lemual broke in. "I can do this, Lander." He squared up to his older brother, and their eyes met. "Trust me, please. I can do this. You're right about Father. You're right about the Third Scouts. I'll do what you say, I will. Just let me do this. I assure you I will not fail. Even if I fail, I won't fall."

Lander shook his head. "I can't lose two brothers."

"You won't," Lemual said. "You'll gain the Drekkers. Trust me."

Lander looked down. Reluctantly, he nodded.

The chief came out, clearly nervous and bearing an odd rounded iron dome with two holes in the top. "Yer headgear, Prince Lemual," he said, handing the piece over. "Now, if ye please," he went on, motioning to Lander and the twins, "the field must be cleared."

After a last bracing look at Lemual, Lander followed Nickel and Winnie off the field to the line of keen spectators. Turning, he saw Lemual slip on the dome helmet, his ears poking through the gaps.

Winnie smiled at Lander. "Very few die from fling-a-ding."

Lander frowned. "Fling-a-ding?"

"Aye. A rock is flinged at the head. If it strikes the iron it dings, nearly blasting the loser's head off, and the match ends. Fling-a-ding."

"How many are seriously injured at fling-a-ding?"

"Quite a few," she replied. "But only if they play close and a face is accidentally struck. The helmet covers only the topmost part of the head. But this'll likely be long range, and, though Haldorn the Hulk there has power unlike anyone else, if they're far enough away the injuries do be far less certain. Does the prince have experience with a sling?"

"No."

"Ah," the twins said at the same time. Nickel nodded. "Well, there's always a wee chance Haldorn, er, misses. I believe he missed once before."

"Aye, true that is," Winnie agreed. "'Twas many years back, but miss he did."

Lander looked over at Haldorn. Donning his

Prince Lander & the Dragon War

own helmet, he grinned across at Lemual, who still had not moved. Both contestants held a sling and had a side-satchel of stones. Lander believed that the stones were of varying sizes, but it was hard to see from where he stood. Haldorn danced around and, even with the heavy helmet, managed a few more flips before the chief came to the center and motioned for silence. Lemual, tiny when compared to Haldorn, still didn't move.

"As visitor and acceptor of Haldorn's challenge," Chief Heckle said, "Prince Lemual Whitson has the honor of choosing the distance of the contest. Prince Lemual?"

Lemual stepped near Heckle. "I choose the nearest possible distance, Chief."

Gasps. Cries. Winnie choked, coughing in surprise. A surge of panic shot through Lander, and he almost rushed the field. But Lemual glanced his way and, amid the worried cries from the astonished crowd, shook his head at his brother.

Chief Heckle was as perplexed as the rest, and his face showed grave concern. How would it be if he oversaw the death of the king's son? He seemed to falter a moment, but recalled to his duty by the growing noise of the engrossed crowd, he called each player to his mark. Lander groaned at the closeness. They were ten paces apart. Haldorn continued to flex his broad muscles and crack every one of his knuckles as he readied himself. Lemual stayed still, his right hand exploring the sack of stones on his hip.

"Contesters, at the ready!" the chief shouted, raising his arm high. Haldorn set his stone—a large one—into his massive sling. The chief shot a worried glance at Lemual, whose sling wasn't loaded yet. "On the cry!" he shouted above the crowd's swelling clamor, seeming desperate for Lemual to arm himself. Finally, he closed his eyes and stepped back from between the two combatants. Grim determination was on Haldorn's face as he set his sling spinning. It whirled with astonishing force, and Lander's heart raced. *How will I explain this to Father?* The chief, with a last apologetic glance at Lander, dropped his arm and cried, "Fight ye!"

Haldorn grinned, and his eyes narrowed. Lemual took a large stone from the pouch and tossed it high in the air above Haldorn. The crowd's puzzled cry came in a wave as many looked up—including Haldorn. When Haldorn looked back down at Lemual, he saw the young prince snag a second rock and hurl it, without the aid of a sling, with great speed. Haldorn tried to dodge, but it was too late.

Ding!

The helmet rang.

Haldorn stumbled back, and the ringing peal at last ended with the huge buck's tumbling crash to the snowy ground.

A momentary pause, then the crowd cheered together. They cheered from some mixture of relief at escaping what had seemed a certain tragedy and approval of the prince's cleverness and skill at hurling a rock by hand.

"Come on!" Nickel shouted, and they took to the field, swarming around Lemual and clapping him on the back.

Winnie stayed beside the baffled Lander, smiling over at him. "There's no rule about how the thing is flinged, so long as it dings!" Some friends were tending to Haldorn, who was out cold.

Lander breathed in deeply, then let out a long, satisfied sigh. "Fling-a-ding," he mumbled.

"Clever," Chief Heckle said, crossing to stand beside Lander. Taking the prince's arm, he went on. "Inventive. Noble. Brave."

"Foolhardy?" Lander asked.

"Probably. But worthy of praise. Worthy of *loyal support*," he said, squeezing Lander's arm.

Prince Lander smiled. "Thank you, Chief. My father will be pleased to hear that."

Chapter Fifteen

Lander slapped Lemual's back again as they turned the last corner before reaching Father's quarters. "You had me very worried."

"I noticed," Lemual said, pulling at the sling he'd been gifted after his surprising victory over the Drekker champion. "When I learned you didn't actually have to use the sling, I thought I had a good chance. I used to spend hours throwing rocks at targets when I was little. Remember when I knocked those pots off Tommie Dunn's head from fifty paces?"

"Oh, yes," Lander replied. "As I recall, Mother was somewhat unhappy about that."

"She disapproved of what she considered to be the danger to Tommie and also the breaking of her favorite clay pots. She was furious!"

"In a royal household," Lander began, and they both finished together: "Every offense is treason."

Laughing, the brothers neared their destination. They grew quiet as they approached the house, suddenly fearful that they would get bad news of Grant. The worst news.

But the look of the soldiers standing guard told nothing of a terrible loss. All seemed as it had been. Lander knew this camp and these soldiers. He knew how to read their moods in their motions, how to sense when something was amiss. Something was wrong, he knew, because of the divide forming over the young bucks' frustration. But the camp right now was as calm as it could be under the circumstances, and Lander was glad of it.

Mother emerged from the door, looking tired and worried. She saw her sons, then exchanged kind words with the guards outside her door and crossed to meet Lander and Lemual.

"My own lads," she said. "I don't like you being away so long. What have you been up to?"

Lander and Lemual exchanged a look; then

Lander said, "Lem was breaking pots over Tommie Dunn's head."

Queen Lillie frowned, accepting a kiss on each cheek from each son. "So, I don't want to know?"

"Probably not," Lemual replied. "But all's well."

Lander took his mother's hand. "Lem has helped Father's cause. He's secured more 'all' for Father's *Defend all, All defend.*"

"That's good," she said. "Everything seems ready to slide down the scale, tipping the balance against us. We must unify here."

"As long as the attack is delayed a little," Lander said, eyes flitting toward the distant sentries, "we can shore up our position here and dig in for a last desperate defense."

"If it's a siege," Mother said, "we won't be able to outlast them. We'll run out of food long before they do."

Lander nodded. It was a reality they had all pondered for many years. Even if they held the line of defense against the initial waves of attack, at some point the inevitable would happen. "How is Father?" Lander asked.

"He is as he has been—perhaps a little worse,"

Mother replied. "He's fretful but otherwise well. He endures. He perseveres."

"And how are you, Mother?" Lemual asked, extending an arm to hug her close.

Tears appeared in the queen's eyes. She wiped at them. "I am well enough. I fear what is coming. I know it is the last chapter for my beloved husband, so I try very hard to be brave for it. I almost wish for him to end his days in doubt over what might happen after he is gone rather than in certainty of failure. He may, at any time," she said, looking into Lemual's eyes, "call on the Third Scouts to embark."

Lemual's face fell, and, breaking away from his mother, he took a few steps back. Looking up with a grimace, he nodded. "I'll do as I'm commanded. But I hate the idea with everything that's in me. I loathe leaving before the great defense, even if it fails—especially if it fails!" He shook his head, then glanced around the camp. "But I'll do my duty."

Queen Lillie smiled sadly at Lemual. "It's because you feel all those things—you think all those things—that you are the right person to lead the Third Scouts away and preserve a remnant of our community. It's a hard job, I know, but it's vital to your father's plan."

"All defend," Lemual said. "Defend all. Except for me."

"It's your way of defending," Mother replied. "It's honorable and loyal."

Lander grieved within. He had lost one brother in the war. He seemed certain to lose Grant as well. Now he faced seeing Lem go, too. It would weaken the defenders considerably because Lem was a good leader and effective fighter.

"Where is Father?" Lemual asked.

Queen Lillie turned toward their quarters. "He was meeting with Captain Walters. He may be back at Grant's bedside by now."

Without conferring further, they walked that way. As they entered the house, Captain Walters was leaving. "Your Majesty," he said, bowing to Mother. "Your Highness; Your Highness."

"Is all well?" Lander asked, sensing something off in Walters' bearing.

"I'm not sure, Your Highness," he replied. "If you please, I think it might be best if you asked your father, sir."

"Thank you, Captain," Lander said, saluting the old buck.

Stepping too quickly, Lander felt a stab of pain from his leg. He winced and clutched at it before quickly trying to resume his ordinary demeanor. Doctor Grimes, gazing over from her seat beside the king, coughed. Her expression was of feigned surprise. "Staying off that wounded leg as I directed, Your Highness?"

Lander rubbed at his leg and gave an apologetic shrug.

Doctor Grimes patted the king's hand, peered at Grant's unchanged face a moment, then turned to leave. Mother reached out and took the old doctor's hand, squeezing it.

"Father?" Lemual asked, drawing close. He didn't need to say more.

King Whitson handed a letter to Lander, and Lemual crowded close to read along.

Lander saw Grimble's name at the bottom and knew what it was.

Mother knew without even seeing. "Grimble wants to meet."

"A summit," Father said, eyes on Grant. "A peace summit."

"Peace?" Lemual asked, doubt plain in his tone.

Prince Lander & the Dragon War

Whitson sighed and turned to his oldest sons. "He says 'peace,' but he means surrender."

Chapter Sixteen

Lander glanced back at the invitation from Lord Grimble, the oathbreaking ally to Namoz Dragonking. The invitation was to what he called a "peace summit."

Lemual coughed and rolled his eyes. "I'm a little suspicious that he may not be trustworthy."

Lander smirked and read the letter more carefully. "Wait, Father. He demands that you go alone and both of you meet far away from your armies on Barren Point, except for one son. He stresses it. Bring a son, or the summit is impossible."

Mother shuddered. "I do not like that stipulation. It hints at some deeper treachery."

Lander clenched his jaw and whispered, "I'd like to get close enough to reach him—with my sword point."

"There's mischief in it," Mother said to Father, placing a hand on his arm and glancing at Grant.

Father took her hand. "Of course there is, Lillie. It's Grimble. He is a treacherous rebel, so we cannot trust him."

"There's more," Mother said.

Father nodded seriously. "I hear, Lillie. And I understand you."

"I'll go," Lemual said. "If you're going, Father, I will go. I want to go. We could go and fetch *Steadfast* from its secret harbor. I'm sure the old ship still floats. We could take it. We can leave Lander here to carry out the defense, in case anything goes wrong."

Whitson smiled at Lemual. "We can't take *Steadfast* to this, Lem. But you're right. Something will certainly go wrong. I'd just like to know how it will go wrong, so I can prepare. So *we* can prepare," he said, looking at Lander.

He already sees me in his place. Lander frowned. "Barren Point is an island this time of year. It's far from the cover of any shore and easy to see from all directions. No one could muster a force too near without being seen. So he's at least thought of that.

Prince Lander & the Dragon War

It's a good place for a summit."

"Aye," Father replied.

Lemual sounded worried. "You aren't going alone, are you, Father?"

"I don't know if we can stand to miss it," Whitson said. "He intends a deception, of course, or simply wants us to surrender and join his side and agree to his gruesome terms with the dragons. He knows we won't ever do that, so there's a trick in it. If we can learn the trick, we might be able to upset things there and avoid the bloodbath that is inevitable if they attack—*when* they attack."

"A trick, Father?" Lander asked. "I have an idea."

"What is it, son?"

"Tricksters," Lander mused. "It takes one to know one."

Whitson blinked. "I suppose...and?"

"I know one."

* * *

The next morning, Nickel Drekker met with the king and his war council, accompanied by Chief Heckle. Winnie chatted with the guards outside.

"A trick's a funny thing, yer Majestic

Gloriousness," Nickel said, coughing nervously as he side-eyed Lander and his chief.

"It's... tricky?" King Whitson asked, smiling.

"Aye, tricks be tricky," Nickel said, coughing again.

Lander passed Nickel a cup of water. "That's why we need you."

"Ye've came to the right rascal with this one, Yer Honored King," Chief Heckle said, gripping Whitson's arm a moment. "Nicky's the most devious scoundrel we've got among us, except maybe that sister o'his."

"She hasn't a tenth of my art," Nickel replied, his tone wounded. He sat up straight and seemed to concentrate. "I'm the one for this sort of caper. Just let me think a moment without hitting me with all yer royal rigmarole."

Lander exchanged an amused glance with Father. The king cleared his throat. "Forgive the rigmarole, young Nickel. How can we help you be comfortable enough to do your best work? Should we leave you to think alone so you can come up with ideas?"

"My Majesty, thanks," Nickel replied. "I've twelve idears so far since ye brought me in—strike that, it's just eight. I had three on the way after I got yer summons. It's not the tricks that are hard. I can think of tricks. I'm just not sure what ye need."

Captain Walters rolled his eyes. "Is this really the best use of our intelligence? The summit is tomorrow at dawn. We don't have a lot of time for—"

Chief Heckle glared at Walters. "Fer Drekker nonsense? Ye don't have time for this Drekker nonsense?" He rose from his seat, his face forming a contemptuous sneer. "I suspected ye would be this way. Come on, Nickel. Our uncouth contributions ain't welcome here."

"Chief Heckle," King Whitson said, placing a gentle hand on the Drekker leader's arm. Then he gripped it tightly. "We haven't always done well in welcoming you to our table, in listening to your story, and in valuing your ways. I'm sorry, and those days are coming to an end. Stay and help us. We need you."

Chief Heckle nodded solemnly and sat down.

Captain Walters bowed to the chief. "Forgive me, sir. I . . . I have my doubts about this scheme. But it's not my place, and I beg you to forgive my outburst."

The chief nodded. "Forgiven and no more thought of. If I'd been told yesterweek that we'd be relying on Nickel here to help us in our hour of need with one of his wild swindles, ye could have knocked me over with a bee's wing."

"Nickel," King Whitson said, "what's your best idea for what we should do?"

"I've got them kind of ideas," Nickel replied, "but it ain't them I think may be most potent."

"Ah!" King Whitson said. "I think I see. What would you do if you were Grimble?"

"Aye," Nickel replied. "That's the way ta think. If he's what I think he is, then he'll be sending a force this evening to rattle us and make us eager to seek peace."

"You think he'll start the assault, Nickel?" Lemual asked.

"Yes and no." Nickel rose and paced the room, closing his eyes and motioning wide with his hands. "'Twon't be the main attack. He'd send a strike force to hit a weak section of our line and let us think twice about what sort of trouble'll come if we won't do his surrender-peace."

Captain Cove nodded, but Lord Galvet shook his head. Captain Walters rose and started

Prince Lander & the Dragon War

to protest but then closed his mouth and shrank back, waving an apologetic hand.

"Dismissing the Drekkers is long in yer line, Captain," Chief Heckle said.

"Probably so," Walters replied, "but I've fought beside you many times, and I never doubt your bravery or skill in battle."

"Aye. We are fierce fighters. But I hope ye will see us as more."

Walters bowed to the chief.

Nickel shot in. "Aye, Cap'n Walters. I hope ye'll see we can also come in with a heap o' deceptive tricks."

Chief Heckle rolled his eyes and shook his head. "Yer the eejit of the world, Nicky Drekker."

A knock came, followed by an officer hurrying in. King Whitson looked up. "Yes, Lieutenant?"

"An attack, Your Majesty! On the northern gate," he said. "Sir, the invasion has begun."

Chapter Seventeen

Lander hurried out, wincing as he went, the pain in his leg keen. He followed the king, who shouted out orders as he jogged ahead. "Walters, secure the central fort, if you please," he called.

"Aye, sir!" Walters answered, saluting as he dashed through the snow.

"Captain Cove, please see that the gate captains are armed."

"Aye, sir," Cove replied, bowing quickly before bolting away with several aids in tow.

Whitson swiveled back. "Chief Heckle, please send half your force to the conflict and position the other half here."

The Drekker chief bowed. "Aye, Majesty. Ye

can count on us!" He turned to Nickel. "Stay with the king, Nicky. Help as ye can with yer tricks and sling."

Nickel thrust his left elbow out and smacked it with his right palm. The chief returned the salute and then dashed off toward the Drekker hold. Meanwhile Doctor Grimes came to Father and was conversing with him quietly. Father nodded. He turned back to his sons. "Lander, lead the defense!" Doctor Grimes touched his arm and motioned at Lander's leg. Blood from the wound seeped through Lander's pants, a scarlet stain spreading slowly over the grey pant leg.

"Aye, Father!" Lander called, spinning to join the bucks rushing toward the northern boundary where the enemy attacked.

"Hold, soldier," Father said. Lander turned back, his face displaying his passion. King Whitson frowned, then nodded to Doctor Grimes.

She stepped forward and drew a long bandage from her bag. "Relax, Your Highness. I wouldn't dare keep you from losing the leg entirely in this fight. I just want to bind it so you can actually make it to the front."

"Thank you," Lander grunted as the surprisingly

strong old doe tied the bandage tightly. She finished, and he darted off. Behind him, he heard Father say, "Now, Lemual, my dear. Do as I say, son, and gather the Third Scouts…"

Lander didn't look back, but he ran on with tears in his eyes. He might never see Lemual or Grant alive again. Wiping at his eyes and taking a deep breath, he steeled himself for what was ahead. This was no time for tender emotions.

Lander charged on, calling out orders and organizing reinforcements as best he could. He came upon a confused knot of young fighters. Lander knew with a glance that they hadn't seen much action. He jogged into their midst. "Who are you, and who is in command here, soldiers?"

A wide-eyed youth gazed up at Lander, and the prince recognized him from the angry gang of malcontents the day before. "Umm, sir. Umm, Your Highness. I'm Riley Nocks. We're in Lieutenant Puck's company, the fifteenth, sir. But he ain't around, and none of us are officers."

Lander pushed down a desire to scold them for their inaction and listlessness. But he knew they were afraid—young, not fully prepared, and afraid. "We can talk through all that later, Riley.

Now is no time for soft talk or debating." He looked the first row of them in the eye in turn. "This is the time for deeds—red deeds. Deeds that bleed."

"Aye, sir!" they shouted, standing straighter and locking eager eyes on Lander.

He went on. "I'm an officer. You may call me Captain Deeds, and you can follow me into the fighting."

A squeaky-voiced buck in the back of the band called out, "Captain Deeds is already bleeding!" Lander glanced down at his leg and then up at the young bucks. Their eyes were wide and their mouths open.

"Want wounds of your own?" he asked, smiling with the challenge. "Battle scars to show the pretty does and those pals who've never respected you?"

"Yes!" they replied, low and gruff.

"Let's get at the battle, bucks!" Lander cried. "Follow me!" They did follow him, running behind and alongside him as he darted through the trees till he came near enough to see the battle lines ahead. "There's the clash, soldiers," Lander shouted above the growing noise. "I need to be at the front of our side before that battle line shifts any farther against us. Can you help me?"

"Aye, sir!" they cried, following it up with a roar.

Lander slid his bow over his head and off his shoulder. He nocked an arrow as he ran and, aiming as best he could, let it loose. It slid past trees and sank into the scrambling enemy line. A muffled scream reached them from the enemy rabbits' line, and the young bucks shouted their delight as the prince nocked another arrow. "Hit 'em again, Highness!" a soldier called, and they drew their swords with another shout, pointing them at the nearing enemy.

Lander squinted intently as he looked along the arrow shaft, pulling back and releasing in a smooth, expert motion. Eyes widening as he tracked the arc of his arrow, he saw a return shot headed straight at his face. He lurched but knew he had no time.

At the last possible moment, a blur of black flashed before him, and a loud clattering sound followed. Lander fell hard, rolling over on the ground.

"Are you hit, sir?" Riley Nocks cried, leaning

over Lander as the other soldiers gathered around their fallen captain.

"I'm not," Lander said, surprised and checking himself over. "What was that?"

The soldiers parted, and there stood Nickel Drekker, his shield raised and his face showing a swaggering smile. "'Twas myself again, yer Sireship. Me shield is yer talisman, I reckon."

"Thanks, Nickel," Lander said, accepting help up from Riley. "Where's Father?"

"I don't know," Nickel replied. "He commanded me ta come foller after ye, and I have—as ye have seen."

"That qualifies you for entry into our unit here, Nickel," Lander said, motioning to the small band of young soldiers. "I'm Captain Deeds, and these are the Mighty Reds—well, now that you're with us, maybe we're the Tricky Reds. But we're aimed at that line up there," he called, pointing at the roiling battle ahead, "and nothing's going to stop us from reaching it!"

They shouted out a war cry as they resumed their run, "The Tricky Reds!" Then they sped on, Lander at the head, flanked by Riley and Nickel.

In a minute they had reached the edge of the

battle line. There was no sign of Grimble himself, but Lander saw elite fighters from the oathbreakers—he recongnized them by the spiral brands on their left arms—leading this attack. Lander leapt into the fight, sword swinging, and was followed by a small but determined band of bucks.

Immediately, young Riley was knocked to the ground, and a jagged pike was driven hard toward his heart.

Chapter Eighteen

Lander lunged, his hacking blade snapping off the spear shaft aimed at Riley. He spun and delivered a kick, sending the enemy rabbit crashing back with a cry. Bending, he pulled Riley up. "Don't look so sad, son," Lander shouted. "You may be wounded yet!"

They set to the struggle. A sizable number of Grimble's soldiers were in this fight. Was it the real battle? Would Grimble divide and attack from various places, opening the way for King Namoz to send in his dragons to complete the conquest? Or was this just the feint Nickel had predicted? Lander blocked a sword swipe from a tall oathbreaker soldier, then leapt over another low strike. His leg felt numb, and he noticed that his leap was not so high as it might have been. He had just missed losing some of that leg that Doctor Grimes was concerned about. He growled and charged ahead.

The young soldiers rushed up around him, striking blows and beating back the attacks of the enemy. Lander saw the enemy commander, a strong fighter named Captain Forne, at the center of the line. Lander parried multiple slashes and strikes, then broke through a thin gap toward the enemy captain.

Seeing him, a cry came from the host of loyalist soldiers. "Prince Lander!" came the shout. "Fight now," urged their officers, "for the Green Ember!"

"The Green Ember!" they echoed, pushing ahead. Lander grinned and thrust high his sword, the emerald gem dancing at his chest as he ran. This delighted his side, but with the sudden press forward of his soldiers, the gap had narrowed.

Lander fought hard to reach the enemy captain, but the surge had made that impossible for now, so he settled into the part of the fight he found himself in. He fought alongside Riley and the Tricky Reds. The young bucks were eager to impress, and many received wounds in the fight. Lander and Riley were beginning to form a good partnership. The eager buck lunged into the path of a sword thrust that would have taken Lander's leg off, and Riley was knocked hard to the ground once again. But he sprang up and beat back the larger enemy, while Lander protected another youngster from a near-fatal mistake.

Nickel was nearby now, blocking with his shield and then striking with his short blade. When he had space, he sheathed his blade and set his sling humming, firing stones into the enemy line. Lander was astonished at how deftly he dealt his blows and how artfully he transitioned between weapons. But he was in trouble now.

Nickel had actually inched closer and closer to the enemy commander's spot, a gap opening around the sling-swinging Drekker as he dashed away at the enemy. Captain Forne had noticed and directed archers to end him. Lander kicked free his own opponent's blade, leaving Riley to do the rest, and darted toward Nickel. Glancing anxiously across at the enemy archers, he dug in and sprinted, then dove—powering off his good leg—and only just leveled Nickel before the arrows zipped through the empty air where he had been. They crashed to the ground amid a fierce advance by the Grimble side. In charged Captain Forne and his best fighters. Lander tried to leap to his feet, but his bad leg failed him, and he pitched sideways, agonizing pain radiating from his wound. Captain Forne grinned as Nickel leapt up and drew his blade too late. The enemy captain hacked away. Nickel was just able to bring his shield around, but he was barreled over, dominated and trampled by the oncoming force. Lander was next.

Forne rushed him. Lander steadied and got to his knees, bringing his blade around to block the first overhead strike, but it weakened his wrist, and the clever captain kicked out, dislodging Lander's blade. Forne laughed, glanced up quickly to gauge the field, and then came for Lander with everything he had. Increasingly crippled and in agony, Lander lunged back awkwardly, barely avoiding the enemy's sword tip slicing across his chest. Lander tried to dive at Forne in the opening after the swing, but his bad leg let him down again, and he crumpled at Forne's feet. The cackling captain gripped his blade in two hands and drove it down at the flailing prince, stabbing it deep into the

Prince Lander & the Dragon War

ground as Lander desperately rolled away. Gasping, Lander glanced along the line and saw at once that his side was beaten back—that the Grimble band had been reinforced, but his company had not. The loyalists were losing. They were going to lose. *I am going to die here, and all is lost.* Forne kicked Lander hard, then dislodged his blade from the dirt and rushed to finish the prince.

One of the Tricky Reds surged in bravely with a well-aimed kick. Forne sidestepped it and kicked back at the youth, then brought his blade down to kill the young buck. Lander raged, staggering to his feet. Swordless, he stood across from his enemy. Fleeing would have been smart, but on his bad leg, he couldn't hope to get away. Attacking would mean a swift, certain end. So he stood there, waiting for Forne to act. Forne would act, and it would mean death.

Chapter Nineteen

Lander was about to die. He closed his eyes as Forne cried out in delight and sliced down on Lander's defenseless form.

Expecting a painful end, Lander heard the pitch of Forne's cry shift from exultant to surprised. A thud sounded, and Lander looked to see the enemy captain crashing back with an arrow in his chest. He was dead.

"The king!" came the cry from the loyalist host. "The king fights for us!"

Lander swiveled back to see Whitson Mariner charge in, bow firing arrow after arrow alongside his band of reinforcements. Casting down his bow as he neared Lander, the old king drew his sword and drove into the enemy. Lander lurched to his feet, watching wide-mouthed as his father fought with relentless ferocity.

"Your blade, Captain Deeds," Riley said, passing the prince's sword back to him.

"Thank you, son." Lander coughed and rubbed his leg. Riley saluted, then waded back into the battle. Lander, after testing his leg and quickly rewrapping the wound, joined in again himself. The prince fought on, but he couldn't keep from watching his father every chance he could. Whitson ended twenty-three enemies that Lander saw, again and again saving the lives of his allies. He fought like the legendary warrior he was, and the oathbreakers were pushed back and defeated.

"They're on the run!" Whitson raised his blade high, and the soldiers nearby cried out, some shouting rude taunts at the retreating oathbreakers. "Lander, lad, secure this area. I must hurry back to be certain they aren't attacking elsewhere in the camp."

"This may have just been Nickel's theory proved right, sir," Lander said.

"Aye," the king replied. "A feint. I believe it was. Still, I must be sure."

Prince Lander & the Dragon War

Lander bowed, and the king held up his sword in salute.

Captain Cove shouted, "A cheer for the king, who's added this day to his long line of heroic deeds. The Savior King!" They cheered him ten times as he hurried off. Finally turning on the edge of the forest, Whitson bowed and waved at the clamoring crowd of weary, grateful soldiers. Then he was gone, and Lander, through misty eyes, turned again to his duty and ordered an officer to take a band and pursue the enemy only as far as the stacked rocks crossroad, then return.

Lander held the north gate, aiding the swiftly arriving doctors as they organized the injured into an order of priority. The prince bent over the worst cases, held hands, and whispered kind words. He had done this for years. It had been done for him. It was the grim duty of all officers—especially a prince.

Later, Nickel Drekker found the prince working to resecure a corner pole on the edge of a hastily made hospital tent. "Yer Highness, the gate's repaired, and Captain Cove said the pursuit party's back and all happy. The enemy's gone. He said yer orders have all been carried out, and ye might inspect the stations at yer will."

Lander grunted as he drove in a peg, then tested its taut cord. "Thank you, Nickel. Tell Captain Cove that I require no inspection. I'll finish up here, and you'll return to headquarters with me. Hurry now. We have more work this day."

Soon Prince Lander was descending through the forest. Reluctantly, he employed a rough-cut staff to lean on, as his leg was hurting worse than ever. Nickel accompanied him all the way, walking slow and talking fast.

When they reached the edge of the buzzing central camp, they saw an unusual amount of hurry and concern. Lander read it at once. Nickel's twin, Winnie, was waiting near the forest. She saw them and hurried over. "Hollie Grimble's gone."

"She ran away?" Lander asked, anger flaring inside.

Winnie shook her head. "I doubt that. She'd been fitting right in here, Yer Highness. I don't know what the officers and lords may say, but she weren't keen to leave. I'd lay odds she was taken."

Captain Walters, seeing the prince, jogged over. "Your Highness," he said, bowing.

Lander glanced at the door to his parents'

quarters. "Sir, my brothers?"

"Aye, sir," Walters replied. "Prince Grant is as he was. Doctor Grimes has a watch on him, even as she treats the cases brought down from the north gate battle. Prince Lemual is with the Third Scouts. They proceed as planned. Your Father—"

"Lemual is gone?" Lander interrupted. "Does Father know? Has he recalled them?"

"Your Highness," Walters said, "your Father is gone too."

Lander dropped his staff. "Gone?"

"Aye, sir. No one knows where he is."

Chapter Twenty

Lander took a long breath and dragged his hand over his eyes. "How long has he been gone? Who was last to see him?"

Walters cleared his throat. "We are getting those details now, sir. I never saw him return from the battle. But several soldiers reported seeing him leave the north gate area."

"I saw him leave myself." Lander frowned, turned back to the forest, and closed his eyes. *Where are you, Father?*

He heard Winnie's voice. "Might he have gone after Lemual and the Third Scouts?"

Lander spun round, then shook his head. "I don't think so."

Mother appeared, walking with a small

company of guards, her face serious. "You know where he went, Lander. A place he couldn't be followed. A place to which only a few know the way."

Realization dawned. "Thank you, Mother," he said, kissing her cheek. To the others, he said, "I'll find him. We'll both be back. Walters, secure the camp. Nickel, Winnie, keep working on a way to deal with Grimble's summit. We must have a way to plan for the certain betrayal."

They saluted, and he was off.

Still using a staff to lean on, Lander threaded back through the forest. He took an abrupt turn west when he approached the north gate and its distant rumblings of activity. Moving down the western slope, he came to a series of caves that ran northward toward a crossroads near standing rocks. He climbed through and came to an impossibly thick tangle of brambles. He followed the edge of the thicket till he saw the small line of brush he was searching for. Looking around to be sure no one was following, he darted into the thicket.

Inside, Lander bent, shoving through the dark brush but careful to break as little as possible. He saw no sign that anyone had been there in a

Prince Lander & the Dragon War

hundred years. He came to a knot of large rocks, sewn together and overrun with wild clinging vines. He climbed a few, then went around others, till he came again to a dense forest with nothing like a path anywhere. And then, he was through it. Sunlight settled on an oval clearing with a solitary tree in its midst. An old rabbit knelt in the snow by a burial site. Lander crossed quietly to stand by his father.

"I don't know what to do, son," King Whitson said. "I used to know so much. But I have learned so much now that I can't be certain anymore. Not about this."

Lander knelt. "Whether to employ the sword in our defense or let it lie?"

"Yes. My heart says I cannot use it—that it's not for me to carry. But my mind knows it would help us defend ourselves against this invasion."

"Shall I carry it?" Lander asked. "I'll risk it in our defense."

"No, son," the king said. "For now, this is my burden. Only the king may carry it. I have clarity on that. You will be king, my dear Lander. But not yet."

Lander looked into Father's eyes. "I would

rather follow you—stay with you, always—than ever be king."

Whitson smiled, and they both stood up. "I felt the same about my own father. He was a noble buck. When we took to the ships on Golden Coast and I was commanded to receive the crown and to lead, I hated more than anything leaving Father behind. He stood on that beach alongside nearly all the older bucks, noble and common alike. I had to leave him there and go on, to carry on and lead so many souls, while he died on that shore. Died for me—for all of us."

"Grandfather was a hero. His memory will never die. I carry him in my heart."

"He would be proud of you, son. He would be so proud of you."

"I know he would be proud of *you*, Father. You have gone so far and done so much."

"Aye," Whitson said, sighing. "I have had a different set of challenges than he faced. I have had to lead and pioneer and innovate in ways he probably couldn't have imagined. I hope he would approve."

"I'm certain he would, Father. You've had to adapt the values you both share to new circumstances he didn't face. You've been a faithful son, a great king, and a wonderful father."

They embraced. Whitson laid his hand gently across Lander's face and looked into his eyes. "Thank you, son. Fleck was right about you."

Lander smiled. "Captain Blackstar was always so good to me."

"Lord Blackstar, if you please, my forgetful prince."

"Ah, Lord Fleck Blackstar Jonson," Lander replied as they stood apart again. "I remember. But he will always be Captain Blackstar to me, shining in my memory of those days. He turned the tide for us. He fought for us. He showed me what it meant to be a soldier during formative days for me. I know it was only a kind thing, but his giving me his Black Star Company patch meant the world to me. It was like getting the Green Ember from you, if you'll allow me to say so."

Whitson smiled. "Of course, I understand that. And it was more than a kind thing. Fleck saw in you what you would one day be. He saw the grown buck I see now with these old eyes. He saw greatness growing in you. And, more importantly, goodness."

Lander grinned, shaking his head modestly. "His oath has helped bind us together as a community. 'My place beside you, my blood for yours.' And he meant it."

"He did mean it. 'Till the end of the world.'"

A cloud glided across the sun and sent a shadow stretching across the clearing. Father knelt again at that moment and took a handful of snow and dirt from the ground. Lander winced as he did, and a nauseous feeling came over him. His eyes glazed over, and he seemed to see a curtain of red, horrified screams, and an endless line of gravestones.

King Whitson turned and, shaking his head, cast the dirt down again. The cloud passed on, and the sunlight spilled again into the clearing. Lander's stomach calmed, and he inhaled a deep, sweet breath, the vision passing. Father turned back. "It's not time. It's not right. I don't know why. I just can't do it. We'll have to find another way. We must hope for an unexpected bequest. I don't know what else to do."

"We'll go down slinging," Lander said. He smiled at his father's puzzled expression. "It's a Drekker saying. I'm getting to know them pretty

Prince Lander & the Dragon War

well. It means that if they are going to die, they'll die fighting—with their slings."

"May it be so, son. As Father and the noble bucks of Golden Coast did. May we fall as we stood—fighting with what strength and wisdom we have for our community and kind."

Lander nodded gravely. "Till the end of the world."

Chapter Twenty-One

Lander and King Whitson found the war council arguing when they returned.

Captain Walters jabbed a finger at Chief Heckle. "I'm not willing to risk his life for one of these mad schemes!"

"Mad Drekker schemes, is it?" Chief Heckle cried back. "What's fer-certain mad is being so conventional that yer as predictable as a sleepy old codger and as easy to defeat as a nattering old nan."

Walters rose, his voice rising. "Predictable? What's predictable is that you're as foolish as you look!"

The chief rose as well, shouting back, "That's over the oval, Cap'n Bellypaunch!"

Whitson walked forward and raised his hand. Seeing the king, they looked around, embarrassed, and then awkwardly stood at attention. "Your Majesty," Captain Walters began. "I, uh…"

"I, uh," Chief Heckle put in, "also, uh…"

Both bucks trailed off, and the king looked at Nickel Drekker, who was leaning back on his chair in the corner, almost to the point of tipping over. "Have a scheme for us yet, lad?"

"Aye," Nickel replied, smiling as he rose and bowed. "A trick. He says he must have His Highness Landerson along for the summit on yon island. So Winnie and me've took a boat that'll bring ye both."

"I don't want to take Lander," King Whitson said. "That's too much risk for this summit. I want to go alone."

Lander listened, but he knew he wanted to go with his father.

"It will appear ye have come alone," Nickel replied. "And if ye won't take the prince, ye can take me. There's room for one in this secret compartment of the boat, where none but yerself shall know at all that ye aren't alone. Grimble'll be surprised when he tries some mischief and ye are suddenly supported by some fantastic sling-swinging warrior—for instance."

"I see," the king replied. "So I row to Barren Point Island, a secluded place, easily seen for miles around, and Grimble does the same. We meet on the island and he thinks I'm alone, but all the while someone is stowed in a secret compartment in my boat."

Nickel nodded. "And the stowaway can see through an inventive little contraption Winnie's come up with."

"Where is Winnie?" Lander asked.

Nickel frowned. "She's right tore up o'er that doe, Hollie Grimble, going missing after th'attack. She feels responsible for letting her get took. So she's trying to find clues to what happened."

"She built the secret compartment in the boat?" King Whitson asked.

"She did," Nickel said, his chin rising a notch. "She's a right hand with a saw, that one. I have the schemes; she lays the beams. I'm imagination; she's implementation. We work well together."

"It's a brilliant idea," Lander said.

"But how does the king get away if a betrayal comes?" Walters asked, indignant.

"*When* the betrayal comes," Lander added.

Nickel held up a hand. "Just calm yer chompers a mo'. Ye haven't heard all."

* * *

Next morning the party stood on the edge of camp, Lillie holding Whitson's hand. Lander had convinced his father to let him go. It was a reluctant concession and seemed to hint at his father's desire to invite him into the decision-making of kingship. Lander would come along as an unseen passenger in the boat's secret level.

Mother Saramack was there. Lander hadn't seen her outside of her secret chamber for several years. She went to see no one. Even the king, who was like a son to her, came to her. But she was there now, her head bowed and her hands clasped together as the first light broke over the camp. Whitson crossed to her.

"Mother, I am so honored that you came today," he said, taking her hand. "Thank you."

Mother Saramack smiled and patted the king's hand. "You're welcome, lad," she replied. "I remember you from long ago, a little buck following his father around. I remember you making

Prince Lander & the Dragon War

your little toy ships and trying them out on the inland lake on Golden Coast. I remember you taking us away, while my husband stood beside your father and the old king himself, and they all stayed behind to fight and die—laying down their lives for us. Heroes all, they were. And you have done more. You have done a harder thing. You lived. You led. You kept fighting when quitting was easiest. You honored them all, caring for their widows—me, even—for all these years. I owe you everything, Your Royal Majesty. I am so grateful for you." She embraced him, patting his back with her thin hands. Whitson's eyes were filled with tears.

Breaking the embrace, he knelt and kissed Mother Saramack's hand. "Bless you, Mother."

Queen Lillie helped adjust the heavy blanket wrapped around Mother Saramack, squeezing her again before retaking Whitson's hand. They walked together toward the gate. "I love you," she whispered.

Whitson smiled at his wife. "And I love you, my dear."

Lander felt the absence of Lemual, of Grant, and even of their other brother, Davis, lost years ago. Heavy-hearted, Lander knelt and kissed Mother Saramack's hand. He waited for some sacred words to come from the esteemed elder of their community. He rose and looked her in the eyes. "My dear Lander," she said, extending a brittle finger to touch his chest. "You've missed a button just there."

Chapter Twenty-Two

Buttons on his shirt all correct, Lander crouched in the boat's secret bottom. Beneath his feet, a rope dangled low and unseen in the water. Ahead, a thin slit revealed their progress as his father's rowing just above brought them closer and closer to Barren Point.

The light was full now, and the appointment was imminent. Father mumbled from above, "I see Grimble setting off from his island."

"Is he alone?" Lander asked.

"No, son. He has Hollie with him."

Grimble had her captured. But to what end? Lander saw them now, as Whitson steered the boat at an angle for a few strokes. The small craft across the river seated two, and Hollie was bound in the stern, a bright red gag around her mouth. The barren island was formed almost entirely of plain rock, with scattered sparse scrub brush giving the only variety. The windblown surface was mostly free of snow, except for packed crevices and white pockmarks dotting the pale grey surface. In times of drought, a land bridge formed on the far side of the River Fay, farther upriver from Grimble Island. But the island was entirely surrounded by frigid water now.

They landed.

"I love you," Whitson murmured so that only Lander could hear. "Don't forget whose son you are."

And now Father was walking toward the center of the small island.

Lander watched Grimble make landfall. He pulled Hollie, who had obviously been hurt in the struggle that saw her captured, onto the island. She stumbled and fell, and Whitson stepped forward, fists clenched.

Grimble drew his sword. "Just you stay on your side, and I will see to what is mine."

"Let you kill your own daughter?" Whitson asked. "Grimble, you used to have some honor.

Prince Lander & the Dragon War

What have you become?"

Grimble grinned. "I hope to become more than either of us ever imagined, son of Whit."

"What has Namoz promised you now?" Whitson stepped closer. "Will he give you a little dragon crown if you slaughter your entire family?"

"You will see," he said as Hollie rose.

Whitson shook his head. "It's not too late to turn away and join us again. We would welcome you back—back home. We could fight side by side and keep the dragons back."

"For how long?" Grimble barked. "A day? A week? The dragons are unstoppable. They have taken this land, and they will hold it forever. They will never be supplanted. There were rabbits here when they came. They drove them out, and most fled southwest. There are still wild rabbits in Natalia who stood where we stand. There are three options: run away and maybe live; stay and die; or make a deal with them. I have chosen the latter. I invite you to do the same—and live! Live on and on!"

"Live in perpetual shame?" Whitson snapped back. "Live as treacherous villains, trading the lives of our most vulnerable for our own security and wealth? Never!"

Grimble gave a short, hacking laugh. "Never say never, Whitson."

Lander squirmed inside the hot closed space. He felt for the latch that would spring open the compartment. He was ready at any moment to rush to his father's side.

Grimble pushed Hollie to the ground.

Whitson seethed. "Leave her alone."

Grimble turned so that Lander couldn't see his face. "You should have brought one of your princelings. It would have been good for you. You're dying, Whitson. Don't bother denying it. We know about your condition. Do you think your army will last without you?"

Whitson laughed. "It will probably be stronger. Lander's a better commander than I am, and half the army is ready to make him king today."

"Not half," Grimble replied, "but many, yes. So you have offered yourself here today because you don't think it will weaken your side."

"If you kill me in whatever mad scheme you've devised, then I believe my army will be stronger after."

"You're that replaceable?"

Prince Lander & the Dragon War

"I am replaceable, yes. But, in death, I will swell in their imaginations, and their outrage at your most heinous act of treachery will fuel the cause of fighting you and your dragon allies for decades."

"It's funny you should mention them," Grimble said, "because King Namoz has offered a solution to our little squabbles over who is the rightful king of rabbitkind."

"We have no squabble," Whitson said, pulling out the Ruling Stone from under his shirt. Lander caught sight of the red ruby glinting in the sunlight as Father stepped sideways. "I am king. You are a traitor. The dragons are our enemies. It's not complicated."

"As ever," Grimble said in his most contemptuous tone, "you struggle with reality. The reality is that I am strong and cunning and have made a more powerful alliance than you have. I am the most powerful rabbit in Natalia. And I will crush you."

"You are a slave, Grimble. Namoz owns you. You are the official taskmaster at his rabbit-slaughtering operation. When you don't work out, he will find another fool to do his bidding. He will kill you one day, perhaps soon, and you will only have lived as a tool to aid his butchery."

"Hard words from a soft old buck," Grimble replied. "But what if I don't die? What if I am made viceroy of all? What if you and I split the rabbit lands and rule as deputies of King Namoz? I think you underestimate his power and, perhaps, his goodwill. You can be a king under him, Whitson. That's all you want, isn't it? A throne? We can have peace, you and I. We can lay down our weapons and be brothers."

"If only we'll accept King Namoz as our ruler and his ways as our ways?"

Grimble shook his head. "We can live largely as we have lived. In fact, we can live beyond and better than we've ever lived."

"What nonsense is this? I am going to die, yes," Whitson snapped. "And so are you, Grimble."

"What if I told you—not for the first time—that you're wrong. I am going to live forever. And you can live forever too."

The water on the edge of the island bubbled, and emerging from beneath the water came Namoz, the dragon king.

Chapter Twenty-Three

King Namoz was flanked by two more dragons, and they all emerged from the water in a strange slow procession. Lander's eyes grew wide, and he fingered the switch to spring open his compartment with one hand while his other squeezed the pommel of his sword.

Water from the dragon king dripped onto the rock as he walked, his mouth opened, and a smoking sizzle came from his lips. His tone was gross and throaty and every *s* hissed. "Whitson the Mariner King, it is you. We have not seen your face for years—since your young Davis died."

Whitson said nothing; he just stood still. A new anger sprang in Lander. Grimble bowed, dropped to both knees, and kissed the rock repeatedly. The dragon king continued, "Rise, Lord Grimble, and aid our sorcerer and priestess with their preparations."

Lander squinted, wiping sweat from his eyes, as the two other dragons stepped to the center of the island, their arms concealed under their robes. Those dripping robes opened at the bottom to reveal that each dark dragon held a black pot beneath. These sizzled with each drip, and steam surrounded them. The tops of the cauldrons were sealed fast by what looked like clay covers. One dragon peeled back a cover, and green smoke billowed out, shrouding the dragons for a moment. Grimble cleared a raised, flat-topped rock of some debris and backed away, head bowed, as the open pot was placed upon it. The green smoke continued to roil around the cauldron's lip, but its thickness diminished. Lander could see clearly again.

The dragon nearest darted a gleeful glance at Hollie Grimble, then bowed to Namoz. "Kart un dumba la hoon rah," it barked.

"Hulla domba Karkon gune," Namoz replied, then turned to Whitson. He sniffed, then grinned grotesquely. "Would your son Prince Lander enjoy

to join us out here?" Lander sighed.

"My son is not a part of this," Whitson replied.

"Then why ever did you bring him?" Namoz asked. "Come, Prince Lander. Your father may not yet know it, but you *are* a part of this. And if you do not come, he will certainly die."

Lander hit the switch, and the secret compartment unlocked. Sweating, he emerged slowly into the cool air. It felt good on his fur, but inside he worried. He took in the scene with a quick sweeping survey. Hollie was being pulled toward the cauldron. The dragon brooding over the simmering pot began a rumbling incantation as Hollie was dragged nearer.

"Come, Lander," Namoz hissed. "See what your father could be."

Whitson stepped closer, hand inching toward his sword. "Do not harm Hollie, or we will be forced to intervene."

Lander reached his father's side and stopped.

Grimble grinned and spat at Whitson. "You've interfered enough."

"We only take a bit of blood. She will live if you do not interfere," Namoz said, scraping

Prince Lander & the Dragon War

his claws against his jaw as the dragon priestess reached gently for Hollie's bound hands. Taking the small rabbit's hand in her right, she darted a knife from beneath her robes and slashed Hollie's arm. Lander stepped forward, but Whitson held him back. "Wait a moment, son," he growled.

The priestess gripped Hollie's wounded arm, shaking it over the cauldron as Hollie's muffled screams mingled with the sickly soothing hisses from the grinning priestess. After a grotesque moment during which Lander was barely able to restrain his rage, the priestess let go of Hollie, and she ran clear of the dragons and her father, straight into Whitson's arms. Lander stepped in front of them and drew his sword.

Namoz cackled. "See," he whined out in a murmuring gurgle, "she is well enough."

Whitson ignored Namoz and looked only at Grimble. He squeezed Hollie closer as she sobbed in his embrace. "This is what you've become, Grimble. Your own daughter's blood given for the savage rituals of these demented monsters! For what? So you can play the petty governor for a few years till they decide to kill you, too? I give you one last call to turn away from this wickedness. Come back to us. Even now, we will welcome you home."

Grimble stepped closer to the priestess as she bent, mumbling dark, wet words while her limbs shot out in sudden, spasmodic jerks. Grimble grinned as he gazed at the priestess. Her white eyes widened, and her twitching head sped into a disturbing rhythm. The sorcerer behind her joined the guttural muttering; his eyes too were wide and white, and his hands rose in looping patterns to punctuate the horrific rise of the sickening ritual. Lander glanced at Hollie and saw Father wrapping her injured arm with a cloth torn from his tunic; then the king swept off his cape and wrapped her in it. Her red gag hung down around her neck, and her slashed bonds lay on the rock at her feet.

"We're going to get you away from this awful place, dear Hollie," Whitson whispered, "and you will have a home. You belong with us."

She nodded, sobbing as he stepped in front of her. The ritual was nearing its end, and Grimble watched with keen anticipation as the priestess stirred the potion. Lander leaned close to Father, whispering, "I have a terrible feeling that if we don't kill Grimble now, we'll regret it."

Father nodded. "I've had that feeling for a long time."

King Namoz stepped closer and nodded at Hollie. "Whitson King, are you a new-hatched youth to sentimentalize some ugly small creature and make it your pet?"

"She doesn't exist for my convenience, Namoz," Whitson replied coolly.

"But she does exist for your inconvenience? You take on burden after burden—the unfathered hatchlings and the deathwives, who all take food and demand protection. Our deathwives are burned with their dead mates as reason demands. But you keep them on into old age! The act of a foolish child. The adult must crush the pet and call the hatchlings back—beating those who won't obey. I must teach you the way, Whitson Underking. You do not live for them; they live for you. You must give your son's blood to me. He will die, but you will live. And if you will drink this cup," he said, sweeping his claws back toward the smoking pot, "you will live on and on, forever."

Whitson stepped back. "I will never drink the deathbrew."

Namoz frowned, a rumbling grumble in his long throat. "It is a potion for never-ending life, rabbitbuck. It is an ancient elixir made from our mossdraft—already a life-sustaining draft—and the sorcerer's secret tincture. He has recently learned, from deep communion in the darkness, that when it is imbued with the spilled blood of the firstborn, it creates power for eternal life!"

Whitson shook his head. "It's eternal death, Namoz. And I will never taste it."

The priestess produced a long, thin goblet from her robes and dipped it through the murky cloud and into the potion. Mumbling, "Dakoo hantun acka raaaash," she handed it to Grimble.

"Don't!" Whitson cried.

Prince Lander & the Dragon War

With a haughty glance at Whitson, Grimble turned back and, accepting the smoking chalice, drank it down in one long quaff. Wiping his mouth, he returned the vessel to the somber priestess, then moved to stand beside Namoz.

The island fell silent, except for Hollie's soft weeping.

Grimble grinned madly and breathed in deep, desperate gulps of air. His breathing grew more and more labored, till at last he fell to his knees, clutching his chest. Lander winced. *He will die trying to live forever.* Grimble's arrogant expression gave way to one of panic, and he looked up at King Namoz in terror. "It burns!" he screamed, tearing at his chest so that his shirt ripped and blood seeped from his frantic scratching. Grimble twisted, lunging at the dragon king and clutching at his arm.

Namoz laughed, casually knocking away the desperate grip. Grimble fell to the rock, writhing in agony as he spun and contorted, legs kicking out and anguished cries echoing over the water.

"We have to help him," Lander said, stepping closer.

Namoz produced a sound, something between

a whistle and a bark, and another dragon emerged from the water nearby. *How many lurked close by, just under the water?* This one wore no robe but bore a crossbow nocked with a thick black bolt. Namoz grinned at the pained expressions on Whitson's and Lander's faces. "For your enemy even? You are so weak that you have pity on this criminal traitor who kills your beloveds?" He laughed, raising his head in delight. "This is why you cannot overcome. Every ruler has obstacles placed by fate and enemies in the path. He must crush them each in turn. But you fashion obstacles for your own path and welcome the obstacles placed by your enemies. You cannot win, Whitson. You are doomed unless you come to our side and drink our cup."

It was Whitson's turn to laugh grimly. "Your so-called potion of eternal life is killing your minion." He nodded at Grimble, who writhed and moaned on the ground. Finally, he began shaking violently. Then it stopped. He gurgled, then lay still, his eyes rolled back in his head. Hollie wept loudly as the sorcerer came near and, drawing a wide black shroud from his robe, laid it over the motionless form of Lord Grimble.

Prince Lander & the Dragon War

"So dies the last son of a once-noble family," Whitson said. Then he whispered to Lander, "Be ready to sprint for it. Remember your bad leg. I'll take Hollie. You just run. There are hundreds of the monsters in the water."

Hollie heard, and she stopped sobbing. "I can run," she whispered.

Whitson gripped her hand. "They took your blood, but not your heart."

Hollie wiped her eyes. "They will pay for it, if they come for my blood again."

Lander smiled, and Whitson nodded.

Namoz laughed again. "You pathetic pets. What must we do to bring you up to our station? We have tried it by our words and our arts, but perhaps you are only fit for food. It was a noble aspiration, though some of my council called it folly. We must crush you, throwing all on Grimble's side. Arming and equipping him and coming for you ourselves—visiting death and destruction on your little fort. We will kill you here and crush them all there! We shall task Grimble Underking to lead the attack, and not one of your camp will be left alive."

Whitson backed up slowly. "How will you

send Grimble to lead an attack when Grimble is dead?"

Namoz uttered another guttural grumble that rounded into a haughty laugh. "You understand so little and love too much, little king. It is you who are dead."

Lander's heart pounded. He glanced from the milky-eyed dragon king to the motionless form that lay covered up beside him.

Lander breathed deep, and he listened for the sound of the waters around them. His ears strained to the possibility of monsters rushing them from beyond the shore. Every sense was tuned to the dangers all around, but his eyes were fixed on the place where Grimble had fallen and was covered.

The black shroud twitched.

Chapter Twenty-Four

Lander gaped. *That twitch happened, right?* He couldn't be sure. Then, again, a small movement rippled the fabric of the shroud.

Lander glanced at Father. Whitson said, "Oh no," just as the shroud shook. The convulsing contortions intensified, and anguished cries came from under the cover. Namoz extended his arms wide, mumbling incantations. The priestess and the sorcerer joined in, all raising their arms wide, their gross throaty chants rising in volume. They seemed to be raising Grimble up, and, beneath the wide cover, he did rise. King Namoz's outstretched hands clenched into fists as the beast beneath the shroud tore it apart!

Lander blinked.

Whitson groaned.

Hollie screamed.

It was Grimble, but it wasn't. He was no longer a rabbit only but seemed to be frozen mid-transition to becoming a dragon. His ears were still long and fur covered, but their insides were scaled. His hands ended in vicious claws and his tail extended, long and powerful. He hunched, neck longer and legs more powerful than any rabbit who had ever lived. Scales wove across his back and on the outside of his arms, while matted fur still covered his belly. He was a hideous hybrid of the two species, and, sensing his new strength, he laughed and clenched his fists in triumph. "I have become a god!"

Whitson backed away slowly while attention was fixed on Grimble. But Namoz swiveled around. The three rabbits froze. Namoz barked at the priestess and sorcerer while the dragon with the crossbow bowed. "Norma kan hooka daynt?"

The sorcerer stepped forward and offered his neck to the dragon king. "Har eefud kolar," he croaked, pointing a shaking finger at Hollie.

Namoz nodded. "His transformation is incomplete because Hollie Grimble lives. My sorcerer says she must die for the rite to be complete—for the evolution to be final. It may be too late now. But we must find out."

Whitson stepped between the crossbow-bearing dragon and Hollie. "Never! She is my ward now."

"She belongs to Grimble Halfdragon," Namoz said, "and he belongs to us. Thus, she is ours."

Grimble stepped forward and tore the crossbow away from the dragon soldier. He grinned at King Namoz, then swiveled to aim the weapon at his daughter.

"Hollie is under my protection," Whitson replied, while the three rabbits backed slowly toward their boat. "We came here under terms of peace, and we demand those terms be honored. Give us safe passage back, as is our right."

Namoz laughed, stepping toward the rabbits. "We do not stoop to your pathetic customs. We have tried," he said, glancing back at Grimble Halfdragon, "to raise you up to ours. But you are a troublesome kind and perhaps should be wiped out entirely."

Whitson growled back, "You have only begun to see how troublesome we can be."

Namoz drew his long notched blade and sprang at them.

"Run!" Whitson cried. Hollie darted for the boat, Lander and Whitson trailing her. A pitched bark sounded from the throat of the dragon king. The water burst with bodies as armed dragons broke the surface and crashed toward the shore. "Into the boat!" Whitson cried, pushing Hollie forward with his left arm while Lander ran at his right.

Just before they reached the boat, Namoz caught up to them. He sent his blade down in an arcing swipe at Whitson, but Lander's sword and his father's crossed and caught the dragon's blade. Lander's heart leapt. Together, they might be able to beat this monster back. Then he saw—he and Father both saw—the clear path between Grimble and Hollie.

Grimble leveled his crossbow and fired.

Lander cried, "No!"

Hollie spun to see the death-bolt shot by her father.

But Whitson was diving sideways, and his heart intercepted the deadly dart meant for Hollie.

Hollie screamed as King Whitson was driven

Prince Lander & the Dragon War

down on the edge of the shore. Lander ran to his father's side and immediately began dragging him to the boat. *There may be time to save him!* Putting aside every thought except getting the three of them away from the dragons, Lander strained. He felt his leg wound tear open but pressed on, shoving from his knees. With Hollie's help he got his motionless father into the boat.

Now the dragons were nearly on them. Namoz laughed and Grimble bounded forward. Lander raised his blade in the face of a hundred dragons closing in. Namoz reached them first and swung his sword again. Lander's blade met it and snapped in half. But while Namoz laughed and drew his great sword back for a final death-strike, Lander kept his broken blade moving. The jagged edge of the broken sword struck the trip-cord that held the boat.

As his dragons swarmed in a frothing frenzy on the shore and Namoz leapt to crush the small craft and the rabbits within it, the boat lurched away.

The pulley system Winnie had designed for their escape was working, and the boat's cable, hidden beneath the hull, was zipping the boat back toward the far, friendly shore.

The dragons raged behind them, and many swam in pursuit, while Namoz and Grimble watched on from the island. Whitson's head lay in Hollie's lap, while Lander knelt over the fallen king.

"Father!" Lander cried, as they neared the north shore. "We're going to get you to Doctor Grimes. We're going to save you."

Whitson coughed and shook his head. Weakly, he tried to pull free the chain around his neck. Hollie helped him. He guided her hands to set the necklace bearing the Ruling Stone around Lander's neck. It was heavy and red with more than the ruby's color alone. Lander wept. Whitson tried to speak, coughed again, then cleared his throat as best he could. His eyes seemed heavy, but he smiled, first at Hollie, then at Lander. He was trying very hard to speak. They both leaned in to hear his last whisper.

"My blood for yours."

Chapter Twenty-Five

Whitson Mariner died on the water, holding his firstborn son's hand while his head rested in the lap of his enemy's firstborn daughter.

"My father!" Lander wept and laid his head on the king's shoulder. "My father, what have they done? Oh, my father."

The boat scraped onto the shore, and Lander lurched with the arrested momentum. Looking up, he saw Captain Walters, Captain Cove, and a band of rabbits rushing to meet them. Winnie Drekker sprinted from the cover of the trees where the pulley contraption had been hidden, Nickel beside her. But they looked afraid. They all looked afraid.

Lander glanced back to the water where scores

of slick forms darted artfully across, spray breaking like a woeful wave. "Fight," he cried, rising and leaping from the boat. "Fight for the fallen sovereign who saved us all on our darkest day. Fight for Whitson Mariner!"

"For Whitson Mariner!" they cried, drawing their blades and lining the shore.

Lander hurried to join them, limping as he went but eager for the fight. Looking at his sword, he saw how badly broken it was. Glancing back, he called for a sword and saw strong bucks carrying Father's body into the forest. Hollie and Winnie attended the fallen king.

A fresh sword was passed to Lander, and he cast down his broken blade. "For the king!" he cried as the dragons neared.

Walters took up the call, "For King Lander!"

The echo came among all the fighting bucks. "For King Lander!"

Lander scowled at them, momentarily unsettled by what had been shouted. He had meant his father, and what they said struck him as wrong. But it was, he slowly realized, right. They were rallying to him—their new king. He tucked the ruby inside his shirt, where it knocked against the emerald already there. He remembered Mother Saramack's words, *You must be who you are.*

Pumping his sword arm in the air, he called out, "To me, bucks! Rally to your king!"

They did. They rallied. The shore was lined by eager bucks, gathered and ready to battle.

Lander just had time to survey his force and the dragons nearing them. His heart sank. Were there five times more rabbits, they would struggle to match well with these monsters. He almost shouted for retreat, but it was too close. The dragons were nearly upon them and would easily run them down in the forest from behind. Their best bet now was to stand and fight.

"Hold a line!" Walters called, and the bucks tightened up, making four compact rows. Lander saw Nickel form up behind him alongside Walters, blades bare and eyes keen on the enemy.

Lander spun back to the water. An enormous dragon swam in front of the others. He reached the shallow water and rose with a roar. He stepped ahead, kicking up water as he came.

"Hold!" Walters called.

Before Lander knew what he was doing, he rushed away from the line of bucks and leapt for the dragon. Entirely surprising his enemy, Lander drove his blade deep into the monster's middle. Lander came down into the icy water, his whole body stunned with the shock of it. The monster clawed lamely at the king, then pitched sideways and died in the gentle surf.

A cheer rose as Lander tore free his blade and spun to meet the next dragon. He came, alongside a wave of them. The line of bucks stepped forward and struck out as the dragons made landfall. Lander battled an agile monster, ducking and rushing close, then leaping to avoid a spinning tail-strike. He evaded death again and again, till Walters and Nickel came to his aid. Nickel blocked a heavy claw-strike with his shield but was driven down with a splash. Lander leapt—forgetfully, this time, from his bad leg—and tripped lamely past the dragon, falling into the frigid water and losing his sword in the swell. But Walters barreled into the beast's middle, driving home his long knife with his left hand, then bringing around his sword with his right. The double strike ended the dragon. Lander stumbled to his feet, both hands free since he had lost another sword, and pulled Nickel up. They helped Walters tear free of his foe, then spun

Prince Lander & the Dragon War

to assess the rest of the battlefront.

It was a horror.

Lander had never seen so one-sided a battle in his life. The dragons were tearing through the brave bucks with ease. It seemed that Lander's bold first strike was an anomaly. Everywhere along the line rabbits were being killed with seeming ease by the evil creatures. He saw only one other injured dragon beside the two he had helped to kill. They had to get out of this, and fast.

A loud signal resounded from Barren Point Island. It was Namoz, the dragon king. It was one of his awful calls, part whistle and part bark. Lander hoped, heart sinking, that it was a call to retreat.

It was not.

In the forest across the water to Lander's left, the woods of Grimble Island teemed with new combatants. They were rabbits! Lander's heart leapt a moment, till he realized, heart sinking, that they were Grimble's soldiers. They embarked in countless boats to join the dragons in their swift conquest of the brave bucks who battled on Lander's side.

Namoz waved at him across the water and dismissed him with a derisive salute. Then he boarded a boat with Grimble Halfdragon and left the scene. It was clear he was saying that this rout of Lander's force was beneath his attention. Lander saw him disappear into the distant woods as the crushing reality set in.

There were no good options for Lander—nor any sudden stroke of leadership genius that could counter these overwhelming odds. The peace summit trap had worked, and the cunning dragon king had forever converted his closest ally to his cause and certainly killed his two most powerful enemies. Namoz had already seen to it that Davis Whitson was killed, that prince who died too young. The living heirs of Whitson very soon would be Lemual, who was gone with the Third Scouts, never to return, and Grant, who was near death now and would certainly die in the days—if not hours—to come. His father's words echoed in his mind, and he felt the full weight of his short-lived moment as king. *I don't know what to do.*

Swordless, Lander turned to the nearest dragon and, shouting out a challenge, rushed to the fight.

Chapter Twenty-Six

Lander lunged at the dragon, but the beast clawed him away easily, pitching him into the cold river once again. He surged up to rejoin the fight, though his shoulder and neck were carved with four fresh lines of red. He stumbled again, crashing to his knees.

"Your Majesty!" Captain Walters cried, stepping high through the shallows at the river's edge. Wheezing, the old captain planted his feet between Lander and the slick beast. The dragon's tongue flicked out as he bellowed a haughty bark and spun, bringing his whipping tail around to undercut Walters' legs. Then the dragon dove in, noxious breath covering the drowning captain in a cloud. Lander rose with great difficulty—his injured leg seemingly useless—and leapt on the dragon's back, squeezing the beast's taut neck with all his strength.

The dragon pitched back, leaving Captain Walters to hobble free, then shook madly till Lander flew off the slippery back and into the water again. Lander looked up from the freezing shallows and saw the boats nearing the shore—boats packed with an overwhelming force from Grimble's oathbreaker army.

The dragon saw Lander's hopeless gaze and laughed a barking, derisive laugh. Snorting wetly, he stepped back a pace, eyeing the coming rabbit reinforcements. They weren't needed. The dragons had torn through Lander's band with alarming ease. The shore was littered with fallen comrades. Lander saw Captain Cove fighting hard near the forest with a knot of determined bucks. Darting his gaze back, he saw the barking dragon surge ahead, claws extended, to tear him apart. With no weapon, Lander set himself to die fighting.

The creature shot out a deadly claw and slashed down at Lander, who made to block him. But the dragon's head snapped back in a startled jerk, and Lander saw two sharp stones sunk into his head, just above his left eye. Lander spun to see Nickel Drekker, sling swinging wide as he sent his deadly projectiles at every nearby dragon foe. It wasn't long till they realized his impact and came for him, knocking his sling free and dragging him down. An enormous dragon was on Nickel. Lander darted to him, snagged the sword of a fallen friend, and hacked at the dragon's back. The scales gave way slowly, but the dragon was not much harmed. Before a final, killing, strike at Nickel, he spun back to challenge the hacking Lander.

"Braan dooka hannum!" he screeched, swiping at the new king. Lander ducked and spun away, grabbing Nickel and pulling him up. Lander's borrowed sword slipped into the river.

"There's nothing for it here, Nickel!" Lander shouted.

"Yer Majesty," Nickel replied, "we must get ye out of here!"

Just then a loud explosion echoed off the water. Lander spun, scanning the river.

He couldn't believe what he was seeing.

"A ship!" he cried. "It's *Steadfast*!"

It was that old ship, left in a secret place upriver years ago, a place known only to the king, the queen, and their sons. It was never intended to be used again. Yet here it was!

Another explosion—this one closer—and the shoreline was riddled with debris from the Grimble forces' boats. Through the smoke, Lander saw *Steadfast* swing toward the near shore. At the prow of the ship stood Prince Lemual, alongside Captain Massie! The Third Scouts must have found Captain Massie's band returning from their errand. Lander's heart swelled with hope. *Could it be?* And then he saw. Beside them, a black-furred rabbit with flecks of grey. A chain of office hung around his neck and from it a medallion of his lordship. The heraldry on his coat of arms was simple. A single black star.

"Ahoy, Captain Blackstar!" Lander cried.

Fleck Blackstar leapt from the boat's prow and waded into the battle, his sword flashing as his soldiers poured from the boat behind him. Lander saw Captain Massie firing his bow at the stunned enemies and Prince Lemual leading a band of Blackstars into the fight on shore.

Lander nearly wept again, this time for joy.

Prince Lander & the Dragon War

Nickel Drekker drew his short blade to protect the king, but the dragons were pivoting to face off against the suddenly more numerous bucks. The oathbreaker band of rabbits, partly destroyed in their boats, swam the icy river for the safety of Grimble Island. Archers on the other side covered their escape. Massie was busy sending arrows into the dragons on the shore.

Lander secured yet another sword from another fallen soldier and rushed back into the battle. The tide had turned. The certain and total slaughter—though still horrific—had been reversed. Finally, fighting through the lines, Lander stood alongside Lemual as they battled a wounded dragon. Lemual swung for the beast's head, but he ducked, and Lander met his chin with a powerful kick. Seeing his middle unguarded, Lemual drove his blade into his belly. The dragon writhed and shot out a deadly claw, but his arm was hewn off by a flashing blade. Lord Blackstar stepped in and, having disarmed the enemy, drove his sword home in the cursing dragon's heart.

Another dragon surged in his place, and the two princes flanked the beast while Fleck

Blackstar came for his middle. A few moments later, the dragon lay lifeless on the shore while the three bucks swiveled to find another fight.

But the contest had shifted dramatically now. The remaining dragons swam back across the water, and there were no oathbreakers left alive on the north shore.

"Your Highness," Fleck Blackstar said, now that the worst bloody work was done. He bowed low on one knee. "Answering your call and reporting for any service you and your father command. I am at your disposal. My army is at your Highnesses' service."

"Thank you, Lord Blackstar," Lander replied. He exchanged a sad glance with Captain Walters, who hobbled up. "We have much to discuss, but this is not the place. Let's return to camp and there hold an urgent council."

"As Your Highness wishes," Fleck said, shooting to his feet. "Blackstar Company, rally to me. To Lener's Crossroads, at once!"

"Aye sir!" they cried in reply and set to work clearing the beach of the injured, helping to transport those who needed it. Most of Lander's band had been killed.

Prince Lander & the Dragon War

"Lem," Lander said, embracing his brother. "Lem, I'm so glad to see you. I feared I never would again."

"So did I, Lander," Lemual replied. "I did as Father said. I left with the Third Scouts. But on our way, we met Captain Massie. He had made it to Kingston and given Lord Blackstar Father's message. They were fully provisioned and on the road that day, and I intercepted them in the forest on their way here."

"An unexpected bequest," Lander whispered.

Lemual nodded. "I was overjoyed. I wanted to honor Father's wish, so I sent the Third Scouts on in the care of Lieutenant Forsythe, and I accompanied Lord Blackstar and Captain Massie back. I thought it might tip the scales. And I led them to *Steadfast* so we could make better time. We split up the force. Some came by the river with us, and some are headed to camp over land."

Lord Blackstar hurried up and embraced Lander. "It's awfully good to see you, Prince Lander. My, you are old now! What a prime buck you have become. Your brother speaks very highly of you. I'm so proud of you."

Lander's eyes filled with tears. "It has been

my dream to see you once again, Captain Bla—I mean, Lord Blackstar."

"I'm still the old captain, sir," Fleck said grinning. "You are still in my Blackstar Company, are you not?"

Lander pulled up his over-tunic sleeve to show a black star patch sewn into the shoulder. "I have never been more honored to wear anything, barring this token," he said, drawing out the Green Ember from beneath his shirt. Then, with a tender hand on Lemual's shoulder, he drew out the Ruling Stone. "And this."

Lemual hung his head, hands darting to his eyes. Lander embraced him.

Lord Blackstar fell to his knees and dropped his sword. "The greatest rabbit to have ever lived is gone. I was too late."

Captain Massie walked quickly up and, bowing to Lander, held out a hand to Lord Blackstar. "The king may be dead, and that is like the forever setting of the sun, but all he fought to defend isn't lost. Not all the light in the world has come to darkness. Let's honor him best by protecting what he loved."

"He's right," Lord Blackstar said, rising with

a grunt. "The dragons won't sleep. They'll be back for blood."

Tales of Old Natalia

Chapter Twenty-Seven

"Long live the king," Mother said, kneeling to the ground before Lander. They were back at camp and in the king's council chamber.

Lander reached for the queen mother, raised her up, and embraced her. "I'm so sorry, Mother."

She whispered close to his ear, "We will store our grief for a season, son. Be what you were raised to be. Be the king they all—*we all*—need. I know you will."

Lander let go of his mother and helped her to the seat on his right at the table. He hovered a moment over what he had always known as his father's chair at the head of the table, then sat in it. The rest sat too. Lander, bloodied and dirty from the battle, leaned forward. "My noble lords, captains, and councilors, welcome. The time we have prepared for—and dreaded—for so long is upon us. The dragons will come, and soon, and we must be ready."

"Defend all!" came the cry from the table. "All defend!"

Lander nodded sternly, a half-frown forming. "I know it was Father's custom to outline the stations of defense at each meeting of his war council, but, given the circumstances, I invite you to speak. Captain Blackstar, my lord, you have governed what has been a citadel of hope under the nose of cruel enemies. I invite your wisdom. I am young and, even as when I was a child, need your insight." Blackstar bowed, and Lander turned to the other side of the table. "Captain Massie, we are so glad of your safe return. You have been my father's right hand through these wars and have been my mentor in many ways. I invite your wisdom at this grave hour." Massie bowed, and Lander turned again. "Chief Heckle, Captain Walters, Captain Cove, Lord Galvet, and all you lords and Mother Saramack. I need your advice. I welcome it."

Captain Walters bowed, then began to speak.

"Your father emphasized the west gate, and he did that because of the approach vector of the enemy. If it's the dragons, mainly, then they will march on us from north and west. So we must be strong there. But as Lord Grimble will hit us from the south, we must be strong there, too."

Chief Heckle nodded. "And Yer Majesty would be wise to look ye fer surprises at the north gate. The villains may hit it again thinking ye won't expect it."

"We must move the bulk of our defense west," Walters said, rising. "The king always emphasizes the west gate, and we shouldn't throw that away—"

Chief Heckle rose, holding up his hands as if to defend from a blow. "Ye aren't accusing me of controverting the word of the fallen king? Surely ye cannot be. We Drekkers'll fight on the west gate like good'ns and die on our feet doing it, but all I'm sayin'—"

"All you're saying," Walters cut back as many councilors got to their feet and began shouting over one another, "is you know better than King Whitson. Well, I can't see that, myself. I served alongside him for years—"

"Enough!" came a harsh shout. The arguing bucks who were leaning over the table and pointing at one another parted, and Lander saw the small, frail form of Mother Saramack. Her ancient face was fixed in a scowl, and she glared at the bucks until they sat down, mute and ashamed. When the room had fallen absolutely silent, she rose and bowed as low as her bent back would allow. Raising up again, she spoke. "Your Majesty. If I may be the first to contradict you, I say that, though you are wise to seek the wisdom of age and experience, and though your humility does you great credit, I do not think it is time for you to be humble." She glanced along the table at the lords and captains. "You all speak of the will of the king, and you mean our beloved Whitson Mariner. Few loved him more than I," she said, touching the queen's hand. "He was like a son to me." Her eyes glistened, but she carried on. "However, with no disrespect intended, it doesn't matter what Whitson Mariner thinks right now. He is not our king. It matters what King Lander thinks." She sat down again, her strength waning. But she continued, "There is no other buck present who knows the layout and tactics of this war better than you,

King Lander. No one knows better which gate to reinforce. You will know what changes to make to the defensive strategy, if there should be any, better than everyone present."

Captain Walters nodded. "She's right. Your Majesty, forgive me."

Mother Saramack coughed. "I have more to say." She cleared her throat and continued, while every counselor listened intently and Lander's heart burned. "What do you think we should do, King Lander? What's in your heart and head? I am older than any of you. My husband fell fighting for this community long ago on Golden Coast. My dear Whitson died hours ago fighting for this community. We might all be dead by dark, fighting for this community. But I am convinced that what my king believes is best. What does he have in his heart to do?" She peered across at Lander.

Lander's heart was full of complex emotions. It felt heavy and proud, carrying his father's memory there. Honor, love, and loyalty were there. His mind felt on the verge of understanding something, and it excited him, but it seemed only just blocked off from his grasp.

Mother Saramack continued. "Hollie Grimble,

my new student, helped attend the return of the body of King Whitson, but she paused in a clearing and watched the beginning of the battle. She told me that she watched you, King Lander. She saw that, when the line formed to hold against the dragons, you leapt forward and attacked the first dragon. Is that so?"

Lander frowned and nodded, and the thing his mind had been trying to find clicked into place.

Chapter Twenty-Eight

The meeting ended, and Lander limped into the center of camp. It was in awful disarray, with posts unguarded and soldiers moving in odd undisciplined patterns. Something was wrong. He felt it, the wrongness there in front of him, but it did not consume him. His heart was set and steady, even expectant.

Doctor Grimes met him, shook her head, and bent to attend to his leg. "Your Majesty, I am sorry to say that many soldiers are packing to leave. A mass desertion is underway."

"How is Grant?" Lander asked.

"Even as he was, sir," she replied. "He may come through, but not if anything…" She didn't have to say it. Not if the dragons overrun the camp.

Walters rushed up, breaking free from a knot of reporting officers. "Your Majesty. It's bad, sir. The army is coming apart."

Lander smiled and nodded. "Understood, Captain. If you please, have the officers gather every buck they can muster here in the center of camp. Say whatever you can to get them to stay at least for this."

"Aye, sir," he replied, and he rushed off.

Doctor Grimes mumbled worriedly as she cleaned and dressed Lander's wound once more. He leaned down. "Good news, Doctor. This is probably the last time you'll have to do this."

She frowned up at him, then bent again, finishing her fresh stitches. She wrapped the bandage tight. "That's the best I can do for now, Your Majesty."

"I feel good as new," he replied, smiling. "Doctor, please bring me my father's memory tonic."

"Your Majesty?" she asked, frowning.

"Quickly now, good doctor."

"Yes, Your Majesty." She bowed and left him, a worried expression on her face.

Lemual crossed over to Lander and bowed. "Please don't send me away again. I want to stay and fight with you."

"I want you by my side," Lander replied. "Only do as I say in every detail, and you may stay."

Lemual beamed, a weight plainly lifted. "Whatever you command, I will do!"

Lander hugged him. "Remember you said that, brother."

"I will," he replied, a sliver of unease creeping into his otherwise delighted face.

"Why did you dismiss the council right after Mother Saramack spoke?" Lemual asked.

"Because I knew then what I was supposed to do, Lem," Lander said. "It wasn't time for talk. It's a time for action. But now I do have to talk—to the army."

Nickel, Winnie, and Hollie appeared, but the Drekker twins stopped at a distance while Hollie approached. She fell to her knees in front of him, and Lemual stepped aside.

"Your Majesty," Hollie said, bowing low. "I am so sorry about your father. I cannot tell you how grieved I am that he traded his life for mine. Mother Saramack says I should honor his act by living a full and virtuous life, but I cannot help but mourn that one so great died for one so unimportant. A great king died for his enemy. It's horrid, and I'm ever so sorry." She wept.

Lander knelt beside her, taking her hands in his. "I understand your grief, and I too feel deeply sad that Father is gone. But if you had known him better, you would be glad of how he died. He died as he lived, really. He would not regret it, so neither will I. Your life has deep value, Hollie. Your only duty is to live well. And the first step is being reconciled with the gift of your life."

"How can I repay such kindness?" she asked through her tears.

"Right now, you must help Mother Saramack secure her chamber. We cannot, at all costs, allow the dragons to have access to our secret lore. They would twist our gifts into unimaginable villainies. They would bend what Fay intended."

Hollie nodded, wiping her eyes. "I will protect the room and dear Mother Saramack. I will die to protect her and it."

Lander helped her up. "Thank you, Hollie. Don't forget to remember that you are alive now. Don't forget to live."

Hollie laughed. "You sound like her—like Mother Saramack."

"That," Lander replied, smiling, "is the kindest word I've had in a long while. Thank you." She bowed and hurried off, while Nickel and Winnie looked on. Lander grinned at them. "What are you two delinquents looking at?"

"Nothing, Yer Majesty," Nickel said. "Only we're wondering what's afoot. The camp were emptying, and now it's filling. Are we coming or going?"

"You will see," Lander replied. He looked around. A large crowd of soldiers had gathered and were packing the open space of the camp. There was a swelling tension among the gathered rabbits, and a worried murmur grew.

Seeing barrels stacked high, Lander began to ascend them. He climbed carefully, trying not to tear the fresh stitches on his bad leg as he slowly reached the top. The crowd gathered close and quieted.

"Friends," he began, "this is a day we will speak of to our grandchildren. We will say, 'That's the day we won an impossible war.' This war has gone on for years. We have been fighting it a certain way, and that has been good. It has allowed us to survive, which was always in doubt. I hear news today that, upon learning of the death of my father, many have begun to pack up to leave. That is a kind of tribute to him, and I thank you for it. Many have learned that the attack we've long known was coming is coming indeed, and they have decided to go. You expect me to condemn you, but I do not." He shook his head and smiled at them. "I say, 'go.' We understand your desire. You want to take your family to safety—away from here to the safety of the woods. I agree with that desire. I do. And I say that every buck is, as of my command right now as your king, discharged from duty to this army. You are free! You may go." He paused, scanning the crowd. "I am forming this day, in this moment, a new army. This is a volunteer army. We would not have you fight beside us if you will not volunteer for it. And I think you should consider it.

"Consider if the woods are safer than this new army of ours. This army will fight between our loved ones and the enemy. Out in the woods, you may find safety. But out in the woods, when the enemy finds you, you will be alone, or in a small band. Here we have banded together. And my new volunteer army will band together and fight like never before. We will protect, as we always have, the most vulnerable. We will fight for the weak and the abandoned. We will band together and be stronger than any of us ever could be on our own. One plus one is sometimes three, because we are better when banded together. I ask you to consider volunteering for my army!" Cheers came from many, and the cheers were swelling when Lander held up his arms and waved them off. "Do not so quickly agree to join my army. I have more to share with you before you decide. I will make it harder to enlist."

"I am with you, King Lander, no matter what!" came an exuberant shout from a soldier stuffed in among a bunch near the front. Lander saw that it was young Riley Nocks of the fifteenth.

"Come up here, soldier!" King Lander called. The young buck scrambled up the barrels and stood on the one just beneath the top of the makeshift pyramid. He bowed and saluted.

"My first recruit," Lander said, smiling. "But he shall be excused, too, after he hears all I have to say. For I invite you all into a danger you have never yet known." A murmur rippled through the host, and puzzled faces looked up at the king.

Lander raised his hand again and continued. "My father's call was Defend all." The crowd shouted back, "All defend!"

Lander nodded. "He trained us to defend our own. He called us to defend. I will defend all we are and have, but in a way my father might never have. I honor my father best by honoring his values the best way I can—in my own way. It will look a little different, but I believe it is the same good cause and the same good hope that motivates my decision."

Another swell of murmuring swirled around the gathered rabbits. Some asked, "Will he surrender?" and another, "Will he follow Grimble's path?" Disagreements broke out, and hot words were exchanged. The most loyal of Whitson's officers, foremost among them Captain Walters, looked at Lander with deep concern.

Walters stepped close to the barrels, disbelief in his expression. "Surely, Your Majesty, you won't surrender to the dragon king?" A fresh surge of groans and shouts of "No!" sounded through the crowd.

Lander held up his hands for silence. When it grew quiet enough, he raised his voice over the crowd. "I will never surrender to Namoz the Destroyer, or Grimble Halfdragon. They can have my blood and bones on the field, but I will never willingly give them an inch. No, my brothers. We will not surrender; nor will we wait here and defend to the end." Lander raised his blade high and shouted, "We will attack!"

Chapter Twenty-Nine

Lander continued over the gasps of the crowd. "That's right, I am attacking the dragons. I know it sounds mad, but it's the best strategy I can think of. It's the only thing that will surprise them, and perhaps unbalance them. I believe it's our only chance. And I will lead whoever is willing to fight alongside me into that last battle."

Lord Blackstar sprang up onto a nearby barrel, his sons Jon and Dane flanking their father. "I will fight beside my king!" A cheer rose from his own soldiers, and many more joined in. "And all my fighting bucks have traveled here from Kingston to fight for our king and his cause. We are no small force already that came by water, but more are coming over land and should be here soon. We will all attack the dragons with you, Lander King!"

The Kingston bucks cried out in agreement. The crowd of local soldiers, awed by the famous but long-thought-lost hero, buzzed with his unexpected appearance. Many had never seen him in person, and they gazed in amazement as if a storybook had come to life before their eyes.

Captain Massie leapt to the top of a barrel and raised his bow. "My bow is yours, my king. I am with you to the end."

"Aye, my king," Captain Brindle Cove called. "I volunteer!"

"I am with you!" shouted Captain Walters. "I am a kingsbuck, and I will go with you wherever you go, Your Majesty."

More rose, all raising their fists or weapons and freshly declaring their allegiance to the king and his cause.

Chief Heckle shouted over a few nearby competing declarers of allegiance. "Aye, King Lander, the Drekkers shall fight w' ye. We shall swing our slings and attack alongside our brothers here gathered. Ye can count on us."

Another cheer. More and more cheers blended together. King Lander, standing on that makeshift pyramid with Riley, Lord Blackstar, Massie, Walters, and now many more, raised his hands one last time for silence. "Listen, friends. We leave in one hour. Report to the same officers you reported to in the last army, but this time tell them you're volunteering for this mad adventure. Officers all, gather your soldiers and then meet me in an hour at this very spot. You'll have your orders, and we will attack. I know we are few," he said, scanning the now quiet crowd, "but we are enough to cause them some trouble. Perhaps a lot of trouble. And in the thick of the battle, who knows what unexpected bequests may come."

Just then, he looked out over the camp and saw a rabbit army marching toward them from the southeast. Captain Massie laughed and, pointing to the marching bucks, shouted, "Here comes Captain Gavin and the rest of the Kingston force. More Blackstars for our fight!"

Lander beamed. "Welcome them in, bucks! Gavin leads them in, the buck who saved my life onboard the *Lillie*. Make way, there!"

They made way, dividing to create a wide gap for the fresh Kingston force to jog through. Gavin, the once-feeble white rabbit who had indeed pulled the young Prince Lander to safety before the ship was destroyed so many years before, knelt at the head of the army. "Your Majesty, we are your servants. We stand ready to follow your commands."

Lander hurried down the stacked barrels, with help from his fellows, limped quickly to Gavin, and swallowed the older soldier in an emphatic embrace. "Gavin!" he cried. "I'm so glad you're here, sir."

"It is a pleasure to see you, sir," Gavin replied, squeezing the king back. They broke apart, and Gavin placed a gentle hand on the king's shoulder. "I am so sorry about your dear father. There will never be another like him. A hero for all time."

"I'm sorry you couldn't see him before the end, but..." Lander said, turning to Lord Blackstar and Massie and motioning them over. When they had joined the small circle, Lander whispered, "Please join me at his grave."

They nodded, and Lord Blackstar said, "We would be honored, Your Majesty, to attend you."

While Captain Walters and the other officers organized the army into the king's strategic divisions, a small band gathered at the north edge of camp, then departed.

Lander led the way, Lemual beside him. Three silent soldiers followed the royal brothers, all members of the old Black Star Company. Lord Fleck Blackstar walked alongside Captains Massie and Gavin.

After a long, winding walk through impossibly dense thickets and over stone boulders, they arrived at last to that oval clearing with a solitary tree in its midst. In an ornate wooden casket, the fallen king lay. Queen Lillie knelt beside the casket, heedless of the snow. A few trusted officers had brought the king's body here, and they stood at a distance, heads hung low.

Lander and Lemual crossed to Mother, kneeling beside her. Lander wept again, and the three of them hugged one another. Finally, Lander rose and spoke softly. "We must go, Mother. I am going to attack them."

Lillie smiled. "Good." She motioned for Fleck, Massie, and Gavin to come forward, and they knelt by the king's casket, paying their respects. Then the five of them closed the casket and lowered the king down into the ground. Shovels in hand, they buried Whitson Mariner near the tree.

Lander smiled. It would be lovely in the spring, when this tree would make for a shady spot. He hoped to see it.

They stood above the grave, and Mother said, "The Prester will come and say the words. We will gather again. We will sing, perhaps. After."

"Yes, Mother," Lander agreed. "For now, go with those officers back to the camp. Go into the mountain and lead those kept there."

She nodded. "I will try to have Grant moved there, too."

"Thank you, Mother."

"Son, an oracle from your mother," she said, gazing at his eyes. "It is a time for fighting. These enemies are not reconcilable. Your father tried with Grimble, but with Namoz, son, there is only one language he understands."

"War and death," Lander said.

"Yes," she replied, taking his face in her hands. "War and death are the words he must hear. Speak to him, son. Speak to him."

Lander nodded gravely. "Yes, Mother. I will obey."

She smiled, tears spilling from her eyes, stared at him a long moment, then kissed him. She crossed to Lemual and had quiet words with him, away from Lander's hearing.

Then she was gone, accompanied by the officers who had waited on her.

Lander turned to his four companions. "We have buried, but now we must uncover."

The others looked at each other, puzzled, then back at the king. "What are we digging up, Your Majesty?" Massie asked.

"An old relic so dangerous my father would never even touch it."

"And do you plan to touch it, sir?" Gavin asked.

"I plan to do much more than that," Lander said.

Chapter Thirty

Lander told them about the starsword as they dug. Lemual had known a little, but the others were almost entirely unaware of the existence of the ancient blade.

Lemual frowned. "So Father was convinced he shouldn't ever use it, or handle it, because he was certain that, if he did, he might kill everyone he loved with it?"

Lander nodded. "That's right."

"And you want us to help you get it and use it now—on the first day you're king?" Lemual asked.

"Yes," Lander replied. "I'm going to use it."

"Are you sure you're right about all this, Lander?" Lemual asked. "The attack plan, the volunteer army, and the ancient deathblade our father was afraid to touch? I mean, are you sure this is the right path?"

Lander scratched his chin. "Of course not, Lem. But it's the best way I know to be faithful to father's way."

"To do lots of things he never would have done?"

Lander nodded. "To be the buck he raised me to be. To be who I ought, with my particular gifts. To work to accomplish what he wanted to accomplish, and wanted me to accomplish, in the best way I know how."

Fleck turned from his digging. "You're right, King Lander. It might not work—probably won't work—but your father, at his best, only wished you to go farther, to do better than him. He would be proud of this bold stroke."

"And if it doesn't work," Gavin added, "we'll all be dead, anyway."

"Really takes the pressure off," Massie said.

Soon they had dragged the wooden cask to the surface. They pried open the top, and Lander gazed inside. The blade was wrapped in a soft blanket.

"Before I take the starsword, here is what we

Prince Lander & the Dragon War

must do," Lander said, turning to his companions. "Lemual and I are going to make a vow, and you three are here to witness it. And, should he fail or fall, you three are pledged to follow through on his task. Do you understand?"

"I think I will understand when you have explained it," Lemual said. "I can't agree to what I don't know."

Lander shook his head. "You already agreed. You said you'd do whatever I command. It was not long ago, brother."

"What is it, Lander?" he asked warily.

Lander produced a bottle from his pocket. "This is a substance that you must keep with you. You must give me your word that you will not give me this bottle unless—*unless*—I voluntarily bury again this blade in a secret place that I cannot access without your help."

"But why can't I give you this?" Lemual asked.

"We are short on time, brother," Lander said. "Do you give your word?"

"Yes," he replied. "I give you my word."

"Say it. Your word to do what?" Lander asked.

"I will not give you this bottle unless you have buried Flint's stone blade in a secret place you cannot access without my help."

"And you three agree to support him, even against me?"

Reluctantly, they agreed.

"Good," Lander said, then drew another bottle from his other pocket. Unstoppering the top, he drained the contents in a long drink. "That was Father's memory tonic."

"No!" Lemual cried, stepping forward. "That's poison, Lander! Doctor Grimes said that would kill you."

"It will," Lander said, "if I don't have the antidote in the next week or so. And you," he said, nodding to the bottle in Lemual's hand, "have the antidote."

Lemual's mouth twisted in anger. "I didn't agree to see my brother die."

"Yes, you did!" Lander replied. "Yes. Yes, you did. You must. It is absolutely essential."

Lander reached into the wooden cask and uncovered the blade. He laid hold of the handle and drew it out. It was smooth and curved back and forth along its edge. Like the night sky, the black blade seemed to sparkle. Lander's eyes widened, and his heart raced. The blade was surprisingly light, and it fit in his grip as if it had always belonged in his hand. He gazed at it with a growing grin, his mind teeming with thoughts of conquest. He felt on fire to bring it to battle.

Then he heard a cough and saw that his companions were staring at him, each deeply concerned. He nodded, then turned back to Lemual. "Will you give me the antidote?"

Lemual stepped back, reaching for the bottle. Glancing at Lord Blackstar, who shook his head, he turned back to the king. "No, Lander."

Lander stepped forward, gripping the starsword tightly. He stared long at the black blade once again. It seemed almost as if he was gazing at the stars on a clear night. He grinned, sighed, then pointed the sword at Lemual. "Give me the antidote, Lem. Give it to me, now."

S. D. Smith

Chapter Thirty-One

Lemual looked over at Lord Blackstar, Massie, and Gavin. They all stepped forward, hands reaching for their blades. "No, Lander. I won't give you the antidote."

Lander gazed into his brother's eyes. He smiled, lowered the sword, and nodded. "Good. That's what it might come to. You have to keep your word, no matter what. You have to stand up to me. This is how we can use this weapon. I alone will bear it, and I alone will die if I don't bury it again. And you must let me die, if I don't have the will to let go of the sword."

Lord Blackstar winced. "It would be too easy for you to take the bottle from Lemual by force. The three of us will bury it somewhere that only we know. We will never tell where it is, no matter what you do."

Lander nodded. "Very good. I will return to camp and await you there. Do as you said and then come to me."

"I'll come with you, Your Majesty," Lord Blackstar said, "and they can tell me later where they buried it."

Lander started to object—felt a deep, keen need to object—but he turned and hurried away with Lord Blackstar. *I wanted them all to go together, because I wanted to follow them and see where they hid it.* He was ashamed, but, fighting down a well of pride, he told what he had planned to do to Fleck Blackstar. He finished, "I hardly even knew what I was doing."

Lord Blackstar listened, then replied. "It's a brave thing to say, sir. And I don't know that I would've had the courage."

"We are about to do a mad thing," Lander said. "I can't let my pride end it all before it's begun."

"Perhaps that's what happened with Flint," Lord Blackstar said.

Lander nodded, and they hurried to the camp.

Prince Lander & the Dragon War

* * *

Lander, having set the bold course of the army, leaned on Lord Blackstar in the officers' strategy session. Fleck, consulting with the king and his captains and lords, made the plan of attack. Soon the army was massed and every officer instructed in his part. Lord Blackstar stood upon a high cart alongside the king and raised his hands for silence. "Good soldiers, it is time." They shouted a cheer. "We take our fight to the dragons, led by our brave king. A long time ago, I pledged my life to him and to his father, to every blessed heir of their line. I had no sword then, but we have a sword on our side that none have seen in battle for ages. I had been forsaken by my dearest friend then, but today I stand beside countless volunteers who are ready to do as I did—to fight for the king and his cause. We will make our oath together, friends!"

They cheered, and the king stepped forward. He motioned for Lemual to join him, and the short prince hurried onto the cart, bowing to his brother king. Lander reached inside his shirt and drew out the two gem-centered pendants. He took off the Green Ember and held it high. "Unless and until I have a son worthy of the inheritance, I name Lemual Whitson my heir. He will bear the Green Ember now." The army was silent, reverent. Lemual bowed again, bending to his knee as he received the ancient emerald. Lander turned back to the gathered bucks. "I am done with speeches. It is time to let our weapons speak. I will only say this: as my father gave his blood for us, so I will give my blood for you. I will live and die for you. Because our vulnerable ones are doomed if we fail, I will not quit this task until we have achieved victory or death."

Blackstar shouted an echo that the whole company joined. "Victory or death!"

"Now, friends," Lander continued, "be brave and keep faith."

Blackstar knelt, and the whole army knelt. Hands over their hearts, they shouted out together, "My place beside you, my blood for yours! Till the Green Ember rises, or the end of the world!"

"My blood for yours," Lander whispered.

* * *

Lander led them, marching back to the riverbank across from Barren Point, with Grimble Island visible on their left. The riverbank was deserted, except for a small advance force of Lander's army, which held the beach and the ship just out in the river. *Steadfast*. As the ship began the long task of ferrying the entire army—in shifts—to the other side, Lander met with his commanders and scouts. "What report of the enemy?" he asked.

The chief scout, sitting beside Captain Walters, bowed his head. "Sir, the dragons are massing on their central mountain. They have seven mountains, as you know, and the central one is where they are gathering. Their stronghold is being reinforced from the southwest and northwest, and they muster their army at its base. It seems all of dragonkind is there. It is a forbidding horde, if I may say so."

Walters coughed. "We had also hoped to be reinforced from the southwest, but we haven't heard from our messengers. Regardless, it is as Your Majesty guessed. The dragons are preparing to attack but aren't prepared to be attacked."

"And the Grimbles?" Blackstar asked.

Walters shook his head. "There are some rabbits with the dragons on their mountain, but they are separated and seem bewildered." The scout nodded. Walters continued. "The oathbreakers' camp is nearly deserted. They seem to have fled, but toward the dragons' stronghold."

"Did you see Grimble himself?" Lander asked the scout.

"No, Your Majesty."

"Do they have their own scouts out, watching for us?"

"None, sir."

"If you had to guess," Lander asked the scout, "when would you say they will be prepared to march out for their attack?"

"Sir, I've watched the dragons for years. I know their ways. I would bet my fortune—if I had one—that they will not march until evening tomorrow."

Lander looked around at his commanders. "Then we attack at dawn."

Chapter Thirty-Two

Lander had slept a bit in the boat that ferried him and his ground commanders to their operations hub on shore, then he slept a little more there. Each time he did rest, he clutched the starsword to his chest. He was wide awake now, peering out into the predawn darkness. His body ached and his leg throbbed, but his heart was already in the battle.

At the king's request, and with his own best selections included, his lords and captains had picked an elite force of the most potent warriors in the army. Lander called them the scalebreakers, because they must scale the mountain and break the line, and because of the dragon scales they must break apart. Many came from Kingston and bore the black star patch, but others were drawn from King Lander's camp and its various specialty forces. He smiled at the young bucks, then turned away, wincing at their eager faces. Few of these hundred soldiers would return alive.

"They know it, Your Majesty," Captain Massie said, and the king knew Massie had read his thoughts. "We told them they would almost certainly die in this company. They all volunteered eagerly."

Lander nodded. "Thank you, Captain," he said, extending his hand. "Before you go, please know how much I have valued your mentorship and care for me, and your loyalty to Father. You have been my most faithful friend, and I have learned more from you than from anyone outside of my parents and Mother Saramack. Goodbye, Captain Massie."

"Sir, I thank you," Massie said, bowing, "but our farewell can wait. I'm coming with you. I'm a scalebreaker, sir."

"No, Massie," Lander replied, "we need you to command the left flank. We need good captains there, and you must be there."

"Sir, the left flank is commanded by Lord

Galvet, a buck who is capable of following the plan and leading his charges," Massie responded. "They are already gone and in position."

"You scoundrel," Lander said, shaking his head and smiling. "It will be good to have you with me, Captain, on this, our maddest gamble yet."

Captain Walters stepped closer. "All is ready, Your Majesty."

Lander frowned. "No, Walters, you should be with the left flank, alongside Captain—" Just as the king was about to name him, he appeared from a nearby trail "—Gavin."

"I'm here, Your Majesty. My place beside you, sir," Gavin said.

"Is this a conspiracy?" Lander asked. "Is Captain Blackstar actually on *Steadfast* with Lemual?"

Massie nodded. "It is a conspiracy, but this is the extent of it, sir. Lord Blackstar and the prince are onboard *Steadfast*, but you tasked us with finding you the best warriors to join you on this mission. And we did."

"You're all rogues," Lander said. "Thank you."

Walters saluted. "The army is in good hands."

"And I am in good hands, too," King Lander said. "The best. Let's do our duty."

S. D. Smith

* * *

An hour later, the sky was a paler grey and the world was more visible. Lander peered up from his hiding place, scanning the dim shapes of the countless dragons covering the side of the high central mountain. In one corner, their grim priestesses droned over low fires, while many dragon soldiers slept by mounds of deadly arms.

Lander rose on his low hill, raising his blade just as the first slivers of sun touched the horizon. "Forward, now," he said. "Let's take that mountain."

Lander hurried ahead, and his scalebreakers followed. He was flanked by Walters, Massie, and Gavin. Nickel Drekker was nearby, too. And Riley Nocks—who the king was certain had not been picked for this assignment but had rather picked himself—marched near the front.

Down the low hill they ran, quietly approaching the dragon mountain. Soon they would hit the outskirts of the camp, so they quickened into a sprint. Lander was in front when the first clash came. An alarmed dragon gurgled in surprise, then leapt at Lander, claws bared.

Lander hewed off the creature's arm, then spun

Prince Lander & the Dragon War

and struck out, splitting the dragon in half with his black blade. Dragon blood sizzled on the edge of the starsword as Lander charged ahead. More dragons came; a noise of warning croaked from a thousand throats and carried up the mountain.

Lander met the first few, hewing them down with a series of astonishing strikes. He struck out, causing several dragons to fall, divided. He saw beyond them the fearful expressions of those dragons farther back who could see what was happening. They clearly feared that all one hundred of the rabbit warriors would be like the first, able to fell dragons with one stroke. It was harder for the rest, of course, but they battled on.

The scalebreakers were driving through the middle of the dragon army. They had made it nearly halfway up the mountain, carving a deep gash in their camp, before the enemy organized and began rushing in from the flanks and dealing death to the invading force.

Lander swept to the left side, dodging a deadly strike from a dragon sword, then hacked his way into a fight in which several young rabbits were pinned down by two dragons. When the rabbits were freed, he helped them to their feet. "Keep at it, bucks!" He did his best to fight the left flank, but as he did, the head of his force, led by Gavin, Massie, and Walters, was driven back. He dashed back to the front and dealt out death among the surging enemy. But the left flank was now losing soldiers at an alarming pace, and the right side was nearly overrun. Nickel was spinning his sling and firing sharp rocks that lodged in the necks and bellies of the dragons. But they had identified him once again as an immediate threat, and ten dragons were converging on him. He fired the last of his ready stones, then hooked his sling at his waist and drew his short blade. The first dragon spun and leveled the young Drekker with his tail. Nickel crashed to the ground, and the dragons pounced.

With a shout, Lander leapt in, slicing two dragons down in an expert attack. He spun and cut down three more, then stabbed and drove back the rest. The last challenger he cut through with a roar.

Nickel got to his knees, touching the wound at his side. Lander protected him while he rose, unsteadily, and resumed his sling. Surveying the scene, Lander realized it was all but lost. His scalebreakers were being driven back and had been reduced by half, at least. Still, they fought on bravely. He saw in the distance that his captains had rushed to the overwhelmed right flank and were striving there against impossible odds. Gavin and Massie teamed up against an enormous beast, fighting for their lives. Just past them, Walters was driven down by a crushing tail-strike.

"No!" Lander cried, but the beast leapt on the faithful captain.

Lander scanned desperately for a way to help but saw in so many places a similar scene. Overwhelmed rabbits battling to their death.

Captain Walters was dead. Half of Lander's force was dead. They had only made it halfway up the mountain.

The dragons were winning.

Chapter Thirty-Three

They came then. Lander gazed past the mass of frothing dragons and saw them charging in. The Drekkers! Chief Heckle led the surging soldiers, their slings spinning and flashing out in a devastating spray. They crashed in on the right flank, firing their stones and pressing into the dragon army. Lander gave a shout and thrust the starsword up in salute to the Drekkers. Every scalebreaker who could join in cheered.

Chief Heckle advanced from the front, his sling dealing death as he came and his force piercing a gap in the dragon line. They fired from their swinging slings till the dragons were nearly on them. Then Chief Heckle shouted an order, and the first line of Drekkers dropped to a knee and

S. D. Smith

drew their blades. Lander's heart missed a beat. The row of Drekkers had extended too low! But the second row of fighters rushed ahead and extended their swords high. Too high! A gap formed in the middle and the dragons were nearly there. Then the third row pressed in between the raised arms of the second and leveled their weapons straight ahead. The dragons hesitated a moment at that thick row of bristling blades. The combat came, though, and the strange brave bucks met the enemy in a fierce clash.

Lander's band, so squeezed a moment before, now felt immediate relief as the dragons had to pivot back and fight a fresher, more numerous force. Lander turned back and saw the left flank charging in now, too, with Lord Galvet in command. The dragons still had superior numbers and strength, but clearly they were surprised by the initial attack and the subsequent reinforcements.

"It's shocked them awake, Your Majesty," Riley Nocks shouted, wiping his face and blinking his wide eyes.

Lander nodded, taking a moment to breathe. "The bad news is that they are now awake indeed."

Riley growled, "Let's put them back to sleep!"

Captain Massie, fresh from killing the dragon he and Gavin had faced, now rallied the right side of the scalebreakers to press ahead and squeeze the dragons there. Nickel fought hard on the left side. Lander rallied the few who were in the middle and drove toward the top of the mountain.

Riley rushed beside him, still somehow untouched by claw, blade, or tail, despite rushing into every lopsided scrape he could join. Lander was beside Riley now and intercepted a death stroke just before it cut the young buck down. Lander darted back, ended the attacker quickly, then rushed ahead again. The king intervened in the fresh clash Riley had rushed in to aid. He made it more than even, and they untangled a knot of deadly dragons and left the cruel killers wrecked and dead on the mountainside.

Though they made a show of stopping the enemy, the scalebreakers let the dragons route around them on either side and soon were topside of the enemy force. Once there, Lander gave a cry, and the gathered armies on each flank swung around to take the higher ground. With Lander at the lethal head of a new, consolidated army, they began to hold their own and slowly push the also now-united dragon army down the mountain. The rabbits had gained the higher ground, and the dragons now fought down the mountain with their backs to the rivers that joined below and behind them.

Lander was the tip of the spear. His faithful

Prince Lander & the Dragon War

captains, along with Nickel and Riley and a few others, protected his back and flanks as he tore through the dragon defense, driving them farther and farther down. He killed countless foes with his flashing black blade. The starsword arced across the battlefield, its appearance meaning destruction for every foe it met.

Lander did not pity the dying dragons. He recalled, as he fought, the many innocents these enemies had murdered. He remembered the grotesque rites of their depraved practice, how they took the young and sacrificed them to celebrate their heinous ways. He remembered his brother Davis, killed in the attack ordered by King Namoz. He remembered his mother, captured by these beasts. He remembered Father, killed by their treacherous cunning. He remembered a catalog of offenses so numerous and consistent that it demonstrated, without doubt, that they were enemies that must always and only be crushed. For the wayward Grimbles, there would always be an offer of peace and the possibility of forgiveness and reunion. For the soulless dragons, there could only be the justice of the swinging sword. And Lander brought that justice in heaps.

Lander held that justice in his heart as he fought, and he battled as none present had ever seen or heard, slaying as he came in terror down the mountain. But still the dragons were so strong, cruel, and numerous that the battle's victory hung in the balance. The line far from Lander always threatened to collapse, and reinforcements were rushed to the front again and again to meet the seemingly endless strength of the dragons. The king drove east and south, always pushing the dragon force as close to the water as possible. He whipped his head back and forth, searching the field for Namoz the Destroyer. He longed to meet his enemy face to face but could not find him.

The battle raged on, unbalancing wildly at times, till the king and his black sword dashed into the gap, sending the dragons flying back and falling by the score. At the water's edge, the dragons regrouped and turned to make a final push to crush the rabbits. But a ship was racing in behind them. *Steadfast*, captained by Fleck Blackstar and seconded by Prince Lemual, surged into the place where the rivers Flint and Fay met. Brindle "Helmer" Cove piloted the ship as it darted across the water near the edge of the shoreline, dangerously close to the shallows. Lander feared it would run aground, but it came around with a spraying wake that dazzled in the morning light. The eager hands aboard quickly sent improvised barrels of blastpowder, already lit, into the midst of the dragon host.

The shattering cracks echoed in deadly succession over the mountains, and the dragon army wavered. Added to the blasts came hails of arrows, shot from close range. Most didn't penetrate the rough hide of the monsters, but many went home in the soft bellies of the beasts. The clever and desperate dragon captains quickly organized a reforming maneuver, and they broke through a line where the rabbits were weak on the southwest side.

But there to meet the dragons, unlooked for and astonishing to see, was a new band of tall wild-looking rabbits, rushing from the trees to form a strong barrier. Lander peered down, eager to see what this meant. "Who are they?" he called, pointing down at the heroic band of rabbits standing against the remaining, reorganized dragons.

Captain Massie sent an arcing arrow into the dragon host, then squinted and stepped close. He smiled, then began laughing. "I don't believe it."

"Captain Massie," Lander snapped, "I cannot make sense of this. Tell me what you see!"

"It's Galt, sir," he replied, pointing at the captain of the wild rabbit band. "See there. He's the one out front with his sword held high."

Chapter Thirty-Four

Lander smiled, but he had no time to ponder the second return of Galt to help them. The one-time traitor was back. He and his band had heroically closed off the dragons' escape.

"With me, bucks!" Lander cried. "Finish them off!"

The exhausted rabbits charged down the mountain after their limping lord. King Lander reached the backside of the dragon host and held up his sword, then his free hand. The armies stopped, and a strange silence fell over what had been a chaotic scene.

"Do you yield?" Lander cried, stepping ahead of his weary soldiers. *This will at least give us a moment to rest.*

The nearest dragon captain answered by ordering a squad of soldiers armed with crossbows to step forward and fire. "Brakkoon dah!" he screamed, and the hail of bolts hurtled toward Lander. The king dove to the ground as the bolts flew, but two still found him. The first bolt sliced his ribs and raced on, but the second caught his collarbone. Feeling a crack, he crashed to the ground and covered his head. His army, with a furious shout, rushed the dragon host. A violent clash ensued, and Lander sat up to watch, just as field medics rushed to attend him. "Patch me up, quickly!"

"Your Majesty," the frightened young doctor cried, "I don't know what to do, sir. You're hurt all over." Lander scowled, then looked himself over. It wasn't only his free-bleeding leg wound or his sliced rib and broken collarbone with a crossbow bolt jutting out. He was an unsightly mess, and it was impossible to tell where his own blood was spilled or that of his enemies. "I'm sorry," he said. "Please remove this bolt." The doctor winced and leaned in to examine it closer.

"Sir," he said. "I don't recommend it. I don't know what will happen if we remove it here. It could kill you."

Prince Lander & the Dragon War

"Understood," Lander said. "Thank you." He twisted so that he could use his good leg and rose with a groan. He tried to heft his sword, but the pain nearly made him collapse again. *If I fall now, I may never rise again.* He switched the sword to his left hand and raised his blade, then rushed back into the battle with a savage cry.

Looking around him, he saw that Lemual and Fleck Blackstar—having left *Steadfast* to Captain Cove's command—were running beside him.

"I thought you'd never come," Lander said.

Lemual smiled. "You've had enough of the glory."

They clashed with a desperate band of dragons on the outside edge of the horde. Crazed, the dragons fought with unpredictable lunges and violent lashings. Fleck moved in, ducking under the wild swing of the fiend's blade. The old buck kicked out against the dragon's ribs, then spun back and leapt over a lashing tail-strike. Lemual swung his blade, which deflected off the wild beast's hide. The beast thrashed back, clawing Lemual away, but Lander drove the starsword in left-handed and ended his enemy. The three warriors cut through the dragon force, finally meeting up with Galt's band on the other side. They had cut the dragon force in half, and Lander saw that many were swimming past *Steadfast* and escaping across the water. Some were boarding *Steadfast* and overwhelming the skeleton crew. Then Lander saw that Lord Blackstar was sprinting back to the ship, a small band of rabbits running with him.

Lander didn't have time to watch, as the battle was desperate in every direction. Lander lunged and cut free the clawing arm of an enemy who was

Prince Lander & the Dragon War

inches from crushing Massie's throat. The faithful rabbit rolled on the ground clutching at his neck but held a hand up to say he would be fine. He coughed and got to his knees, while Lander waded back into the furious contest. Lander felt exhaustion pulling at him, and he knew his soldiers must be nearly dead with it. He had done far more work than any other, but his blade was special. It weighed almost nothing, and he felt alive with a wild fire while he held it in his hand—even his far-weaker left hand. He felt unstoppable.

His bucks were stoppable. And they were being stopped. He dashed to the aid of Riley, pinned down and kicking up uselessly at a cackling dragon. Lander arrived, and the dragon never laughed again. "Are you okay?"

"Fine, Your Majesty," Riley said, grinning. He pointed at a long red trench across his face where a dragon's claw had no doubt found him in the fight. "Is it a good one, Your Majesty?"

Lander nodded, smiling wearily. "It's perfect." Reaching for Riley's hand, he made to pull him up but crumpled to his knees with the agony. He had forgotten and extended his right hand and, though he could squeeze, it came with horrendous pain. Riley leapt up and, seeing the bolt lodged between his king's neck and right shoulder, cried for a medic. Lander shook his head and got painfully to his feet again. They fought together a while, Lander battling on desperately with his left hand and several times nearly losing his life to protect Riley. Seeing Captain Gavin struggling against a wounded dragon, he darted over to help.

Wherever there was a desperate case, Lander rushed there, rebalancing the battle over and over with his deadly weapon. But he was losing so much blood, and his energy was draining away. *I cannot win through this, but I can see that we win.* Stealing a moment to glance toward the river, he saw no sign of Lord Blackstar but watched as *Steadfast* got under way. A wild battle on the deck caught his eye. Lander thought he spotted the old buck on deck fighting bravely amid the chaos, but the king was quickly distracted from that by a closer encounter. Lemual cried out in pain, and Lander spun to see his brother one-on-one with a huge creature driving at him with a pike. The pike went home in Lemual's side, and Lander shouted, stumbling as he reached his brother just in time to help him overcome the determined dragon.

Prince Lander & the Dragon War

Another dragon raced up and drove his pike home in Lander's left arm. The king cried out, barely holding his blade, then spun back and made for the dragon. Lander tripped into the enemy, then swung an ineffective slice that tore something further in his throbbing left arm. The dragon bent beneath the blade and countered, delivering a crushing punch to Lander's jaw.

Black. A stuttering blackout, followed by flashes back and forth of light and dark, striped and sideways views of the battle flickering off and on, till he hit the ground hard.

"Lander?" Lemual asked after—after how long? He wasn't sure. "You all right, brother?"

"I'm dead," Lander answered, blinking.

"You're not," Lemual said, leaning down to help him up. "Not just yet. I know you're weary and wounded, brother. But you must see this."

Lander winced. Lemual's tone was not joyful. Lander stood slowly and tried to shake his mind clear. His head ached with the shaking, and he snapped his eyes closed and clenched his jaw tight, hoping to somehow hold it all together. He blinked and opened his eyes and saw that the field was clear of standing dragons. They had won this battle. His heart surged with a sudden, hopeful longing. He glanced down and saw that his black blade was sheathed at his side. They *had* to be finished fighting. Had to. Lander was certain he had nothing left to give. His arms felt useless. He was faint with blood loss and wasn't sure he could remain upright for very long. He knew his army was desperate for rest and reinforcements. He winced at Lemual. The unspoken question passed between the brothers. *Why are you concerned?*

"There," Lemual said, nodding north as he leaned on his sword. Captains Massie and Gavin gasped for air nearby. Lemual shook his head. "The big mountain."

A secret cave had been opened halfway up the center mountain, and the dragon king, Namoz the Destroyer, was marching out with a fresh hoard of dragons behind him.

Chapter Thirty-Five

Lander reeled, barely keeping his feet. They had fought so bravely, and the audacious strategy had seemed to work. But in the end, it had failed. He had failed. Namoz wasn't among the many dragons they had sacrificed so much to defeat. He was there now, with his best, freshest soldiers, and they would rout the ragged army of exhausted bucks.

"Where is Captain Blackstar?" Lander asked.

"On the ship, Your Highness," Massie managed between deep breaths. "He pursues the enemy."

Lander pivoted to see *Steadfast* across the confluence of the two rivers, near the far shore. It was on fire. The fire rose amidships, and Lander stumbled toward them. "They've got to get off the—"

An explosion, a rending blast, followed by a quick succession of others, blew the ship apart. *Steadfast* was, in a terrific, fiery finish, completely destroyed.

It was the blast of doom, an echo of woe that resounded in Lander's heart.

He gazed at the burning wreckage, the far-flung debris, black and bathed in orange as it pitched onto the hissing snow. Lander fell to his knees. *My father. Oh, my father. My father's friend. Oh, my captain!*

Amid the groans and gasps of the nearby soldiers, Massie knelt by the king. "Your army needs you, sir. One last effort, then we can finally fall and rise no more. If you cannot lead us, sir, I will do my best."

Lander shook his head as tears fell from his eyes. "I am here." He stood, with help from Massie, and began to march back to the mountain.

As the king passed, each exhausted rabbit knelt and bowed, hand over his heart. They could see. They knew what would happen when they reached the mountain. Still, they knelt. And when

Prince Lander & the Dragon War

the king passed, they fell into line. They knew they walked to their doom, but still they followed. A long formation of battle-ravaged rabbits marched behind their king.

At last they came to the mountain. King Namoz waited at its bottom, in front of his army on the wide, soggy plain before the river's edge. The snow had been trampled into mud, and the hardy dragons waited behind their master. Lander saw Grimble Halfdragon just behind Namoz, but his heart did not hate. Weary as he was, and knowing that the traitor's own murderous crossbow bolt had killed his father, he felt pity for Grimble in this moment. Grimble would be on the winning side today, but he would lose everything in service to the evil lord he had chosen.

Lander limped out in front of his own battered band and waited. It was clear who was in charge of this encounter, and it wasn't the rabbit king. Namoz said nothing, only set aside his crown and his robe and strapped on his long notched sword. Another blade was strapped on his back. Then the dragon king stepped forward, away from his army. He walked straight toward Lander. Reaching the halfway point between the gathered armies, the

S. D. Smith

Prince Lander & the Dragon War

dragon king stopped.

Before he had really thought it through, Lander walked ahead. He tried not to stumble or limp too significantly, but there was no hiding his condition. It was plain to all. He thought hard, with what cleverness he had left, how he could possibly face off against this giant long-time king—this fresh and focused enemy. Lander was none of those things. He was a small half-dead rabbit who had ascended to the throne only the day before. His reign would be brief, but memorable. The king who lost all. Maybe some surviving scholar from the Third Scouts would record his name in their histories. Alas. He had more immediate concerns than the assessment of future scribes. He had a fight to die in.

Neither arm worked properly. He knew he could not swing with his left. In fact, he could not feel his left arm at all. And his right arm—the memory of that agonizing moment when he had last tried to use it stuck with him. The crossbow bolt jutted from his collar, and it pained him to even think of making it worse. He stared across at Namoz. *What would Father do?* he asked himself. The answer came fast. *He never would have been*

Prince Lander & the Dragon War

here, because he would be back defending the camp, like he did for so many years. "Since he's not here," Lander unintentionally said aloud, "I guess I'll have to do what *I* would do if I were here. Since I *am* here."

Namoz tilted his head in a question, then smiled greedily and watched Lander walk all the way out to meet him. They stood ten feet apart. Namoz said nothing. Lander said nothing. The rabbit king just breathed deeply, trying to silence the questions in his mind—trying to search out what strength he had left. What cunning. The well was low, but not altogether dry.

Namoz said, "We will kill you now, little king. We see you have slaughtered our gathered hosts, and we are amused. But do not, little lord, rejoice overmuch. There lies hidden in our stronghold—that stronghold wherein we did certain rites in preparation for battle while you visited us, un-looked for—a certain doom for you. There sleep the seeds of this fallen army replenished a thousand times over. We only need wake them. And we will wake them and make the world our own. You have stalled our project a little while, but the end will still come. We leave this mountain to take every mountain. And you will be a hazy memory, a mist that vanishes at dawn."

Lander eyed him coolly. "I feel like a pretty good nightmare. A memorable one that shakes you awake. Have you seen me in your dreams with my black sword flashing? One day this blade will break, and every enemy will be defeated."

"You will be broken this day."

"Maybe so."

Namoz growled a throaty challenge that needed no words to understand. Lander felt its menacing warning thunder deep inside him. The host of dragons clattered their weapons together and repeated the guttural growl.

Namoz drew the second blade from his back and clashed the two together, producing a high-pitched ring as he repeated his throaty challenge. A rattling rumble followed, and he bent into an attack posture with his feet spread wide. "Defend yourself!" he roared.

Lander shook his head. "You first."

Aiming all the focus he could find on ignoring the roaring pain, Lander ran at the dragon. The dragon king's eyes widened a fraction, and Lander smiled through gritted teeth. The rabbit king

Prince Lander & the Dragon War

reached with his right hand for the starsword, and with the last of his strength he gripped and ripped it free. His wound complained with astonishing pain, but he ignored it for now and rushed the puzzled dragon king, who stepped forward, then back, and flung out his twin blades with a cry.

Lander made a vague show of wanting to slice sideways but brought his blade around to strike down at the dragon's locked blades. The starsword tore through them both, cleaving them so that the stunned dragon stood gazing at his two broken swords. Lander wasted no time but stepped closer, seeming to stab at his enemy's belly. Namoz pulled his middle back and his hands, still clinging to the sword hilts, shot forward. But Lander wasn't stabbing. Turning in an agonizing twist, he swung his blade high and, with a roar, took off the dragon king's head.

Chapter Thirty-Six

Lander tottered, and Namoz fell.

The rabbit army cheered, and the dragons quavered. Cheer followed cheer, and the bucks surged ahead, rushing to fight the last of the dragons. Lander felt them fly past him, renewed in their energy and hope. After many had rushed by him, he fell to his knees, dropping the starsword. It lay there, whole and unbroken, and Lander wept. He had hoped so much that the ancient blade would break. If he had the strength, he would have tried to break it on a stout rock. But he had felt it in his hand. He knew it, in a strange way. In a strange way it called to him to pick it up again. To use it to do, in a good way, what the dragon king had planned to do. To go from this mountain of astonishing victory and conquer the world. It was an alluring call.

Lander fell to the mud, and, eyes trained on the black blade only a few feet away, he faded.

* * *

"Your Majesty?" Captain Massie asked, touching his shoulder. He seemed far away to the king but grew closer as he went on. "Sir? Will you sit up, sir? You're in the mud." Fading, Lander saw Massie split into pieces and roll up into the sky in flashes that finally flickered to black. "I've looked for you, sir," Massie said, back and in view again, "but I was locked in pursuit of Grimble. That was a fool's errand, for no one could catch him. He's faster than any creature ever seen."

Lander sat up with Massie's help. Massie wiped some mud from the king's face. Lander squinted against the pain and reached to rub at his eyes. The agony was intense, and he let his arms fall back to his sides.

Captain Massie drew closer. "Are you well, sir?"

Lander shook his head, and tears stood out in his eyes. "I don't think so, Captain. I'm afraid of what may come..." He trailed off suddenly, head darting around, looking for the starsword. "Where is it? Oh, no! It's fallen into enemy hands. Grimble has it! He'll kill us all and conquer the world!"

Massie held up his hands. "No, sir. No," he said, soothingly. "That's not true, Your Majesty. Look there." Massie pointed at the king's scabbard. In it was sheathed the starsword.

"How?"

"A friend, no doubt," Massie replied. "It is a terrible threat, sir. I think I understand how much."

"It cannot be kept," King Lander replied. "It cannot be at hand."

"You are prepared to do as you promised?" Massie asked.

"That, or die," Lander replied.

Massie nodded, then turned back. "Medic, there! A doctor for the king, at once!"

The doctor came; in fact, a small team of them came. They cleaned and stitched, patched and anointed the king. His pain eased somewhat, and the bolt was successfully removed. He was bandaged up and given salve for his pains. He did not argue, only accepted whatever they asked him to do. In time, he faded into sleep again, leaning against a rock. He was once again awakened by Captain Massie's voice.

"Sir, we have many duties to perform. Many weighty things to be decided. Your officers and lords are working, but they will soon need your voice among them. But first, you must eat something—and drink." Massie unbundled and laid out a small field ration meal and convinced the king to eat a little and, with help, to drink a good amount of water. The water was green-tinted and tasted strange. Massie said they had gotten it from inside the mountain. *Is this poison?* Lander didn't care. He drank and drank.

Lander began to feel a little better. He rose, with help, and walked slowly ahead. Soon they reached the entrance of that cave from which the dragon king had emerged. Inside, countless eggs covered the ground. A dripping fountain fed a green-hued pool in the corner. He gazed at the strange water. *They call it mossdraft*, Lander recalled from the conversation with Namoz on Barren Point. It was invigorating.

He shuddered.

Prince Lander & the Dragon War

A hasty council of lords was meeting near the pool. Lander knew what they were debating before he heard a word. He listened for a while, offering no comment, but hearing both sides of the argument articulated clearly.

Lander agreed with both sides.

He met Massie's questioning gaze and shook his head. He felt a strange certainty that clarity was close. It was discoverable, if only he could lay hold of it. It was near, though, he knew. But he also was certain he couldn't find it here—not in this dank tomb.

Without saying a word, he left.

Chapter Thirty-Seven

Massie Burnson followed the king at a discreet distance.

There could still be a stray dragon or two on this mountain, and Massie wasn't about to let King Lander out of his sight. He left the dragon egg chamber and took the same path upward as the king. A messenger from their camp appeared and ran over to him. He saluted and handed Massie a note.

Massie's heart sank. The worst may have happened. While they were away, the Grimbles raided the camp. Or it was dragons. He tore it open and read, prepared to be alarmed.

He smiled.

Looking up, he hurried after King Lander.

The king was weary, he could easily see. Massie almost considered running up to him and insisting he come down from the mountain and rest immediately. But it wasn't Massie's way to insist on anything where the king was concerned. He never had with Lander's father, and even though he had virtually helped raise the young prince, he wasn't about to insist on anything now. But he did follow and came closer as the king climbed higher.

As Massie ascended, he sometimes lost sight of the king around a corner. The battle had been thick up here, and he passed grim evidence that the fight took more than dragon lives. It was a sad scene, but he could not help but be glad at its outcome. It was an astonishing—impossible—victory. Massie believed he would never see another battle so glorious however long he lived. He hoped he wouldn't. He hoped this was the end of his time fighting. He hoped it was the beginning of an endless age of peace. He looked down on the busy rabbits scattered down the mountainside, all doing whatever they could to help the injured and exhausted. Goodness was being practiced throughout the army. He smiled at it, always delighted to see that his community was so often more eager to heal than to fight; they were more loving in service than terrible in war. Lost in his thoughts, he forgot himself. Turning back to the mountain path, he could not see the king. All he could see was smoke, and he smelled the grotesque presence of the dragons' dark rituals. He ran.

Massie hurried to the top of the central mountain, where Lander Whitson stood amid a ruin of smoking rocks. The stench of death hung in the fetid air.

"Sir," Massie said, dropping down to one knee. "The lords await your decision."

"Captain Massie," Lander said, his strange faraway gaze on the river below and the forest extending from each bank into an incomprehensible distance. "This wood is great, I think. I look at it and seem to see our kind thriving here."

Massie rose and turned to take in the spreading forest. "Yes, sir. The wood is vast and uncultivated. It would require tremendous work."

"It will be my life's work," Lander said, unblinking eyes gazing off to the horizon.

Massie passed his hand over his eyes. "Sir, the decision?"

Lander turned to Massie, but his eyes kept their peculiar look. "We must bury the threat and our best weapon against it together."

"What will we do?" Massie asked, eyes closing tight. "It will be too easy to find."

"We'll dam the river, build up our warren, and make this mountain forbidden. We will try to forget."

"But sir, what if the worst happens?"

"Then one from my line will remember. And when the time comes, he will rise."

Chapter Thirty-Eight

King Lander came down the mountain and gathered Prince Lemual and Captains Massie and Gavin. "We have much to discuss. First, I have decided to bestow on you, Massie Burnson, a new rank and title. You will remain a captain, but you are now a lord as well. Lord Blackstar became a lord and is no longer a captain, in fact, though he is called that. You are the first Lord Captain."

"Your Majesty is very kind," Massie replied. "I'm honored, sir."

Lander smiled at his old mentor. "You'll be less honored when you find out all I have planned for you to do."

They smiled and congratulated Lord Captain Massie. Then the king began to tell them of his plan to build a new warren in the great wood surrounding the confluence of the rivers Flint and Fay. He explained his idea of damming the river and letting a lake swell to surround the mountains where the dragon eggs would be left to sleep. Inside that secret and forbidden mountain, he would also bury the starsword. "But," he said, "I feel there must be some way to unbury the blade when it is needed. The trick is to keep it safe until that time. We shall have to ask Mother Saramack for her counsel. But I feel I have the outline of what we must do. Tell no one of this."

Prince Lemual nodded, absently fingering the emerald gem around his neck. "Many of the lords are demanding we collapse the mountain in on the dragon seeds and end their threat forever."

Lander frowned. "Maybe they're right. But until I have clarity on another way, I proceed with my plan."

Gavin bowed. "We are with you, King Lander."

King Lander turned to Gavin. "Lord Blackstar's sons? Have they been told of what happened? And what of Galt?"

"Lord Blackstar's sons are below. Dane is hurt but will recover in time. Jon is well, and he is assuming command of the Black Star Company for now. I will assist him, of course, and I will go with him back to Kingston when the time is right—if Your Majesty gives me leave." Lander nodded, and Gavin continued. "Galt, we have learned, was with Lord Blackstar. They were seen on the ship, fighting side by side. They fell fighting together. Galt's widow is here with us, and his oldest three sons, too."

"Extraordinary," Massie said. "My old captain and his lieutenant. Gavin and I were just lads when we were asked to join them. It was such an honor. I can't believe they are gone."

King Lander nodded solemnly, touching, with intense pain, the black star patch he always kept on his shoulder. "We lost many faithful bucks today. Captain Walters fell, he who was my father's right hand and as faithful a buck as ever lived. We have lost too many."

"We will toast them," Lemual said, "when we share that drink together. The cider, with a special ingredient."

"We will," Lander said. "I will do my part."

Massie stood quickly. "Your Majesty, I almost forgot. I got word from camp that your brother

Prince Grant is awake and talking."

"What?" Lander and Lemual said together.

"Aye, sir," Massie replied. "Forgive me, but I lost the message in all the madness. Give you joy, sir. Doctor Grimes wrote the note herself."

"A happy message, indeed," Lander said. "And we should all of us be happy. This is the end for so many of us, but it is a beginning too. It is a beginning that these heroes who lie here fought and died for. A beginning unlike anything we have ever yet known. I can feel it, my friends. We will build something here that will last into a bright and beautiful someday. And more than homes and roads and gates and towers, we will build a kingdom that defends what is good. We will build a way of living and loving where we protect the vulnerable and value one another. We will keep faith with the cause of always aiming at the mending. We will focus our hearts on hope."

Epilogue

Two soaked and battered rabbits washed up on the shore of Flint River.

They lay there a while, unconscious. "Have we survived, after all?" Galt asked as he came awake, coughing as he rose to all fours.

Fleck jerked awake. He gazed around, eyes wide, then crawled farther up onto the snow-covered beach. "We may have, old friend."

Clear of the icy water, they collapsed on the snow. Fleck Blackstar reached out and laid his hand on Galt's back. "You stayed, old friend."

"We stayed," Galt replied. "Together."

They sat up, breathing deeply and exhaling large clouds of misty breath. They had jumped from *Steadfast* just before it exploded. Across the water, rabbits of all kinds were rallying around the king. Lander was coming down from the mountain, flanked by Captain Massie, Captain Gavin, and Prince Lemual. "Now he has a chance," Fleck said. "We have a chance."

"You were always faithful, Fleck," Galt said. "You never wavered."

Fleck nodded, smiling. "Oh, I've wavered many times. But I've had a good life so far. My story isn't over yet. Still, somehow, I like your story better—there's a lot more drama."

Galt barked out a laugh. "I suppose so." He gazed at the celebrating rabbits, their cheers echoing across the confluence of the two rivers, the Flint and the Fay. "Will they be okay, do you think? Will we?"

"I think there are many troubles ahead—many trials and tearings," Fleck replied, "but in the end, I believe we will find our mending."

"I hope so," Galt said, getting to his feet.

Fleck gazed through misty eyes at the scene unfolding around the king and his army. Seven times they cheered King Lander, led by Gavin and Massie, and Fleck saw his son Jon Blackstar, alongside Prince Lemual. Fleck smiled wide, clasping his hands together with joy.

Then, as the cheers died down, Massie knelt and placed his right fist over his heart. His left he used to grip and raise his blade. Then they all knelt around the king, fists over hearts, many raising swords in imitation of Captain Massie.

Fleck knelt in the snow, right fist over his heart. With his left hand he reached for his blade. His hand closed on nothing.

Swordless, he prepared to join in the familiar, beloved vow.

Galt stooped beside him. Kneeling in the snow, they shouted out the vow together.

"My place beside you, my blood for yours! Till the Green Ember rises, or the end of the world!"

The End

S. D. Smith

Prince Lander & the Dragon War

About the Author

S. D. Smith is the author of *The Green Ember Series,* a middle-grade adventure saga. Smith's books are captivating readers across the world who are hungry for "new stories with an old soul." Enthusiastic families can't get enough of these tales.

Vintage adventure. Moral imagination. Classic virtue. Finally, stories we all love. Just one more chapter, please!

When he's not writing adventurous tales of #Rabbits WithSwords in his writing shed, dubbed The Forge, Smith loves to speak to audiences about storytelling, creation, and seeing yourself as a character in The Story.

S. D. Smith lives in West Virginia with his wife and four kids.

www.SDSmith.com

About the Illustrator

In seventh grade, a kid sitting behind Zach Franzen in music class reached into a ziplock bag of pencil bits and hurled some pieces at his head. Zach whipped around and threw his pen at the assailant. It turned once in the air and stuck in the boy's forehead. This is a true story. An onlooker, desiring to confirm what he witnessed, repeated, "It stuck in his head." These days Zach seeks to use his pen, pencil, or brush to create images. Hopefully, these images might have force enough to stick in the heads of those who see them.

Zach lives in North Carolina with his wife and their daughters. The Franzens love to drink tea, read stories, sing harmonies, perform in plays, paint, eat (but not eat paint), and take walks.

www.ZachFranzen.com

Want to be first to get news on new *Green Ember* books, S. D. Smith Author Events, and more?

Join S. D. Smith's newsletter.
www.SDSmith.com/updates

No spam, just Sam. Sam Smith. Author.
Dad. Eater of cookies.

Green Ember **illustrator Zach Franzen created these beautiful coloring pages.**

When you give S. D. Smith five, they are free for you to download as thanks for your support.

www.SDSmith.com/gimme5

Want to listen to the Green Ember Audiobooks for FREE?

Request to borrow through your library on

**Or with no wait
IF YOUR LIBRARY HAS**

hoopla

Visit the S. D. Smith Store for new Merch, Books, Downloads and more!

The Green Ember Series All Books Bundle (Softcover)
$87.99 $114.88
ADD TO CART

Helmer T-shirt - (All SIZES: Youth Small - 2XL)
$16.99 $19.95
Youth Small
ADD TO CART

GREEN Oath T-shirt - (All SIZES: Youth Small - 2XL)
$16.99 $19.95
Youth Small
ADD TO CART

Heather's Necklace
$11.99 $15.95
ADD TO CART

Picket's Sword
$21.99 $24.95
ADD TO CART

The Archer's Cup (Green Ember Archer 3)
$10.99 $12.95
ADD TO CART

Ember's End: The Green Ember Book IV - Softcover
$12.99 $15.95
ADD TO CART

Green Oath Hat
$22.99 $25.95
ADD TO CART

www.SDSmith.com/store

The Green Writer

Try 3 FREE Writing Lessons from S. D. Smith at GreenWriter.SDSmith.com